"Look, Su

l

"Then kindly let go of me."

"If I do, will you promise not to run away?"

She looked into his eyes. "Okay," she said slowly, "I promise."

True to his word, he released her, allowing a momentary feeling of truce to pass between them. Suki swallowed nervously. He was very, very sure of himself. He was devastatingly attractive as well.

"I still can't figure you out," he said. His eyes swept boldly over her petite figure, assessing her.

Suki raced for the door, and would have made it if she hadn't lost her balance. She had the door halfway open before he slammed it back shut.

"Oh, no, you don't. And you promised me."

"I had my fingers crossed." Suki was in a panic. "Let me go or I'll scream."

"Go right ahead." He smiled, challenging her with steely confidence. "No one will hear you."

She opened her mouth, but before she could let out a good healthy scream, he leaned forward and covered her lips with his . . .

Diana Morgan

Diana Morgan is a pseudonym for a husband-and-wife team who only moonlight as writers. By day they are two of New York's busiest literary agents. They met at a phone booth at Columbia University in 1977, and have been together romantically and professionally ever since.

"We began writing together strictly by accident," they confess, "deriving our pen name from our cat, Dinah Cat Morgenstern." Writing turned out to be a welcome form of comic relief from the pressures of business.

"This is a wonderful opportunity for us to talk directly to you, the reader. Our books have often been described as humorous or zany, but we feel there is an underlying seriousness to even our craziest story. What we hope to convey is a certain joie de vivre that will escape from the pages into a part of your life. Whenever we accomplish that, we feel like a million bucks. If we do, please write to us in care of SECOND CHANCE AT LOVE and let us know."

The "Morgans" enjoy all kinds of music, pigging out, small children and elves (especially their daughter Elizabeth), and trying to figure out what will happen next on Dallas.

Other Second Chance at Love books by
Diana Morgan

ANYTHING GOES #286
TWO IN A HUDDLE #309
BRINGING UP BABY #329
POCKETFUL OF MIRACLES #354

Dear Reader:

Escape from all the holiday hustle and bustle and lose yourself in these six compelling stories from some of our finest writers...

Martina Sultan's *When Lightning Strikes* (#376) is a sparkling tale of love at first sight conquering seemingly formidable obstacles as New Yorker Jenny Weber meets Colorado cowboy Cooley Jameson. Advertising executive Jenny can't imagine life without the bright lights of Broadway and the world's best cheesecake, but when Cooley saves her from drowning, his Robert Redford looks turn her head so fast she almost forgets there's a Central Park! Yet she knows she can never be the woman he needs. Martina Sultan draws on her own creative advertising background for a firsthand glimpse into that exciting world.

That trademark—Diana Morgan's humor—is in top form in *To Catch a Thief* (#377), a madcap crime caper featuring two million pilfered dollars—and irresistible romance. Unspeakably sexy private detective Fletcher Colman finds the hot money in artist Suki Lavette's suitcase. Only—as Suki tries to tell a skeptical Fletcher—it's *not* her suitcase. The sinister Donald Luchek is stalking Suki—even as Fletcher's accusing her of being Luchek's accomplice—and a punk-rock musician bashes her favorite sculpture. What else can go wrong? The banter flies fast and furious as this dynamic duo's zany adventures propel them toward the delightfully romantic conclusion.

You readers know that the Kay Robbins name signals a surefire hit, and *On Her Doorstep* (#378) is no exception. When reclusive author Erin Scott finds city slicker publisher Matt Gavin literally on her isolated cabin's doorstep, she runs him off with a shotgun blast that sends his horse careening down the mountain. But Matt's intrigued by Erin's diamond-in-the-rough manner and the caged fire he sees flashing behind her green eyes—and not even the dragon of Erin's painful past can keep this persistent knight from claiming his lady. Intense emotion and terrific dialogue fuse into powerful passion in this, Kay's latest triumph.

In *Violets are Blue* (#379), Hilary Cole poses the classic question, can you ever really go home again? When successful TV actress Maggie London returns to her small Missouri hometown, hoping for a break from her hectic career, she's stunned to find herself coerced into playing opposite her high school sweetheart, devastatingly handsome NFL quarterback Alex Graham, in the community theater's summer show. Tension builds with Maggie's fear that their stage roles can't conceal the one love she's never recovered from—or her startling eight-year-old secret...

The age-old theory that opposites attract takes on new meaning in *A Sweet Disorder* (#380) by Katherine Granger. "Tidy" Tracy Holliday has made a name for herself as a management consultant specializing in neatness, and she hopes to pick up clients at a Boston newspaper convention. But Wade Montgomery hardly fits her image of the typical harried editor—he's messy but gorgeous, and she's not sure where a "consultation" with Wade might lead. When Wade asks for a week of Tracy's "Neat & Orderly" services at his paper in a tiny New Hampshire town, there's plenty of sexy, disorderly debate before this relationship gets all straightened out!

It's romance at sea in a glorious Alaskan setting in Kasey Adams's *Morning Glory* (#381). Investment counselor Amber Daly is trying to assess the shaky financial standing of Captain Dan Anderson's beat-up old freighter, but she's finding the captain less than cooperative, and Amber's sure he's hiding something. Still, the cold Alaskan winds are no match for the fire of passion this rugged sea captain sets in Amber's heart, and their isolated on-board existence rapidly turns attraction to longing, as Amber struggles to uncover Dan's secret sorrow...and to come to terms with a ghost from her own past.

So, happy holidays—and happy reading!

The Editors
SECOND CHANCE AT LOVE
The Berkley Publishing Group
200 Madison Avenue
New York, New York 10016

SECOND CHANCE AT LOVE™

DIANA MORGAN

TO CATCH A THIEF

TO CATCH A THIEF

First edition published December 1986

First printing

Printed in the United States of America

Second Chance at Love books are published by
The Berkley Publishing Group
200 Madison Avenue, New York, NY 10016

TO CATCH A THIEF

- 1 -

"TWO HOURS IN VAIL, COLORADO, and already three things have gone wrong." Suki swung her oversized pocketbook onto the front desk, forcing the hotel clerk to duck. He just missed being clobbered as it landed on top of the bell, which rang with a muffled clang.

A bellhop promptly appeared and picked up her suitcase. He glanced at her sleek form, clad in a short black knit dress and black stockings, with low-heeled black pumps that strapped at the instep. Her hair was pulled back into one long black braid that swung freely from the very top of her head. With large, expressive green eyes, slightly tilted as a legacy from her Japanese grandmother, Suki peered back at him from a smooth ivory face. He returned her questioning smile and held the suitcase up, evidently in order to get a clear view of the strange pyramid with the eye in the middle that was painted on its side.

"That's not my luggage," Suki explained. "Mine looks the same," she continued helpfully, indicating her odd-looking suitcase, "but that's not it. I took this one by mistake at the baggage claim at the airport, and I didn't notice that the name tag wasn't mine until I was in a taxi." She pointed to a crisp card attached to the handle, where a name and destination were printed. "I believe the owner of this bag is registered here."

The bellhop examined the bag again and nodded his head. "Mr. Donald Luchek," he announced. "I just took up this exact suitcase not more than five minutes ago to his room, 1607." He gave the luggage another curious glance and shrugged. "I can't believe there'd be two of these."

Suki paid no attention to him as she turned back to the desk clerk. "That solves problem number one. Now tell me why, after I killed myself getting my sculptures to Vail in one piece, your men haven't delivered them here yet? I've got a showing tomorrow night in this hotel." She sighed. "This is the last stop on a rather exhausting tour. I've been to five cities so far, and nothing has gone wrong. Maybe a perfect record was too much to ask for."

The clerk maintained his cordiality. "Your sculptures will be delivered here tomorrow morning. Conditions on the highway are very dangerous, and management felt that, due to the fragility of your works, we should wait for the roads to be cleared to avoid any accidents."

Suki nodded, relieved. "That does make sense. Thank you."

"We did manage to have your policeman brought over separately," the desk clerk continued. "I took the liberty of setting him up myself by the Jefferson Room." He pointed all the way across the lobby, where, sure enough, a plastic true-to-life sculpture of a cop with a gun drawn stood poised for action. Next to the sculpture was a sign advertising tomorrow's exhibit.

Suki watched, amused, as a passerby flinched when he saw the policeman. After a double take, the man examined it cautiously. Finally, after ascertaining that the policeman hadn't budged, he slowly reached out to touch it. A surprised laugh of relief ensued as he realized he had been duped.

"I must admit, I had the same reaction when I first saw it," the clerk told Suki. "I can see why the style is called Photorealism. It looks so—real."

"Thank you," Suki said hurriedly, not wanting to get into a discussion with the clerk. People always had the same reaction to her work, and just now she was very anxious to get up to her room and into a hot bath. "But let's get back to my third problem, okay?"

"Which is?"

"My room reservation. Where is it?"

"But you never made one."

Suki was stunned. "But—but you knew I was exhibiting here. Isn't it all automatically . . . ?"

The hotel clerk shook his head emphatically.

Suki pouted, her wide green eyes growing even larger. "Is there anything you can do?"

He smiled and nodded. "We have a guest leaving

a day early." He gestured to where a young girl sat with a brand-new leg cast stretched out in front of her. Crutches lay on either side, and now skis and luggage sat in front of her. "Her misfortune is your good fortune."

"Three for three." Suki smiled triumphantly, but her exultation was short-lived. A sudden crashing sound made her turn in time to see her sculpture go careening across the front of the Jefferson Room.

The object that had hit it was an amoeba-shaped guitar case being lugged by a purple-haired youth in a black leotard with a tiger-striped tattoo running up the side of his left arm. He was followed by three other equally adorned beings bearing the logo PURPLE SLUDGE on the sides of their instrument cases.

Suki and the clerk rushed over and examined the damage.

"I thought I bashed a bobby," the musician said in a guttural British accent.

His friend bent down and examined the damage. The statue's derriere was completely broken off, revealing the hollow interior. "It's a bloody sculpture," he announced, surprised, but he eased back when he saw Suki glaring at him. "Oh, uh, sorry, miss, Slime here didn't mean it no harm."

Suki picked up the broken piece and examined it with a frown. "It's fixable," she sighed. "Luckily I brought along my repair kit." She threw up her hands in defeat. "Which, unfortunately, is in my suitcase."

The purple-haired musician, apparently the head of the group, apologized again. "Tell you what, now." He fished around in his pocket and pulled out two tickets. "Here, take these."

Suki looked at the tickets. "Orchestra seats to the Purple Sludge concert."

"It's the least we can do, seeing as how we banged up your copper and all," his friend said. "No harm done now, right?"

Suki looked at the paper-clip earring that hung from his ear. "Uh, no, no harm done, Slime."

"No, he's Slime, I'm Mud. The bugger over there with the skins is Grease, and that's Ooze, our lead guitarist."

"And I'm Suki." She looked at the broken piece in her hand and sighed again.

"There's a tool shop on the top floor that you can use," the clerk said, apparently trying to be helpful.

"There you are, that sounds smashing," Slime said. "And we'll be glad to help you carry the copper up there."

Suki put up a hand to stop him. "Don't bother. I'll feel safer doing it myself." She reached out and took the sculpture under her arm. "But first I'll attend to Mr. Luchek and my luggage."

"Luchek?" Slime was interested. "You mean Donald Luchek?"

Suki nodded. "You know him?"

"Sure do. He's our manager. Swell chap. He's a big producer, and he's handling our first concert here in Vail. Are you a friend of his?"

"Uh, no," she said dryly, "we just share the same taste in luggage." She readjusted her purse on her shoulder, and at that moment the strap chose to break off. The bag dropped to the floor and Suki mentally counted to ten.

"The day's not even half over," she said to herself. "What else could possibly go wrong?"

Suki counted each floor in the elevator as it headed up to the sixteenth. She was generally not a patient person, preferring life to move quickly and without hesitation, and she was already behind schedule.

"Come on, come on," she muttered. "Let's go." She was all alone, the wrong suitcase still in her hand, the six-foot sculpture of a cop holding a gun propped next to her, and the derriere piece tucked neatly under her arm along with her purse. She double-checked the piece to make sure it was in good shape just as the elevator came to a halt. The statue teetered slightly, and she steadied it as the doors opened.

Her impatience went on hold as she regarded the man standing before her. He was the picture of commanding elegance in sleek navy blue and gray, and his restless energy matched her own. His eyes were a startling shade of deep blue, keenly intelligent and wholly alert to everything around him. Suki stared unabashedly. He was the most alarmingly magnetic specimen of male she had encountered in a very long time, even more attractive than Chad Norton, the magazine-perfect aspiring actor who had left her a year ago for a role in a hot daytime soap opera. She had written to Chad faithfully at first, but he had quickly lost interest as he became immersed in a lifestyle that was as unappealing to her as it was foreign. She had been blindly, worshipfully in love with him at one time, thinking he would be the next Robert Redford and Dustin Hoffman rolled into one. But even her loyalty had finally cracked when, after eight months apart, she had visited him in L. A., only to find a shallow, self-involved shell of the man she had once loved. She hadn't expected ever to meet anyone who could rival Chad in looks, however, at least not so soon. But now this dynamic stranger who fairly radiated vitality was looking straight at her, and she groped for something intelligent to say to him.

But he made the first move. His eyes lit on the cop with the gun, and he instantly froze and raised his hands.

"Don't shoot!" he exclaimed. "I'm unarmed."

Suki restrained a laugh. "It's okay," she said reassuringly, her smile a bit tremulous as his disconcerting eyes met hers. Did he effortlessly unravel every woman he met? She took a deep breath and gathered her poise around her like a cloak. "It's only a statue." She tapped the cop's head with her hand, and it made a hollow sound. "See, plastic."

"A statue," he repeated wryly, sounding almost disappointed. "I was held up by a statue?" He arched one dark eyebrow. "I hope this isn't the start of a dangerous trend." Holding the doors open with his foot, he examined the policeman more closely. "It looks so—"

"I know, real," she broke in. "Right?"

"Exactly. Rather like Madame Tussaud's wax sculptures in London." Transferring his keen gaze to her, his eyes lit with an appreciative glint. They traveled subtly downward, taking in her sleek, graceful figure, only partially camouflaged under the black knit dress, and then returning to her sylphlike face. Suki didn't know why she wasn't outraged or embarrassed by his casual perusal of her, but she wasn't.

What was even more baffling was that she was glad he had noticed her. She shifted her body slightly in a silent acknowledgment of his recognition of her, feeling suddenly as if she had jumped onto a roller coaster. Their eyes met for a second longer than was necessary, and she stumbled, bumping against the statue. If there was a walking illustration of charisma, this man was definitely it. She swallowed hard, trying to appear cool. It wasn't easy. He carried an aura of absolute power, but he carried it easily, as if he had been born to it.

He stepped inside the elevator with compact grace. "Which floor?" Suki asked, glad for an excuse to speak to him.

His shrewd eyes glanced at the button panel and snapped instantly with surprise. "Same as you," he said. "Sixteen." His gaze transferred to her again, this time with alert curiosity, and stayed there.

Suki shifted from one foot to the other as the elevator ascended once again. By now she should have been unnerved by the way the handsome stranger was boldly staring at her, but for some reason she found it intoxicating.

The elevator came to a stop and they both stepped out, Suki lugging the statue with her.

"Allow me," her companion said at once, deftly catching the policeman under one arm.

"Thank you," she said. "This shouldn't take long." Suitcase in hand, she lumbered down the hall, letting him follow behind, until she found Room 1607.

"Hello in there, Mr. Luchek," she called as she knocked with her foot. "Are you in there?" She felt a tap on her shoulder, and when she turned around, he was leaning against the wall with his arms folded, a knowing smile on his face.

"Look no further," he said.

She gaped in surprise. "You're not Donald Luchek, are you?"

He paused for a tiny fraction of a second. "Why not?"

She held up the heavy suitcase she had been carrying. "I think it's time we made the switch, don't you?"

"The switch?" He spoke easily, but she was all too aware that he was still watching her like a hawk.

"This is your bag," she explained. "With all that craziness at the airport, it's a wonder we got our luggage at all."

He frowned for a moment, as if piecing it all together. Then his face lit up and he sighed in apparent relief. "So that's where it was."

"Of course," Suki continued. "And now, if you'll just open up and get me my bag, I can be on my way."

"Oh, of course. Let me just get my room key and . . ." He reached into his pocket and fished around, coming up with a surprising assortment of odds and ends, including a rabbit's foot, several marbles, a woman's hairpin, and a pair of dice. It seemed like an unusual collection for such an elegant man, and Suki looked at him uncertainly. "I'm afraid I must have left it in my room," he said. "I'll have to go downstairs to the desk."

Suki frowned, slightly puzzled. He looked like the last sort of person to forget anything—and yet why would he lie about his key? She picked up the rabbit's foot impulsively and dangled it between them. "You're not superstitious, are you?"

He laughed, a warm, resonant laugh that made her blink in surprise. His fingers closed around hers, grabbing the rabbit's foot so that it stopped swaying, and their eyes met. His touch was warm and strong, sending a delicious tingle up her arm. "Take it," he said, amused. "Perhaps you need it more than I do."

"Uh, no, thanks," Suki said, flustered, and placed it back in his hand. "I don't believe in—" She leaned back against the door, and it opened suddenly with the force of her weight. Falling backward into the room, she landed on the floor with a thud. The policeman fell with her, and she managed to save it by letting it land on top of her. She looked up, totally disheveled, and saw him standing in the doorway holding the suitcase, gazing down at her.

"Are you all right?" he asked, stepping forward to help her.

"I'll live."

His strong arms lifted her up, and she fell back against his hard, unyielding chest. For a moment, they stood together, Suki leaning against him, and her heart leaped irrationally as his hand slid down her arm. Then he pressed the rabbit's foot into her hand. "I think you'd better hold on to this," he said dryly, but his voice was edged with humor.

Suki let out a frustrated breath. How mortifying. Now he probably thought she was a klutz as well as a careless type who took other people's luggage by mistake. Hiding her embarrassment, she reached for her statue and moved it safely back into the room. Looking around, she saw that she was in the lavish sitting room of a very expensive suite. "Wow!" she said. "This place is like a sultan's palace. All it needs is a harem."

He lifted an eyebrow but said nothing, closing the door and double-locking it behind him. After dropping the suitcase, he began to look quickly around the room with an intensity that puzzled and frightened Suki. He moved with a lazy grace that belied his sparkling alertness, as if he were about to conquer a kingdom but would do it in his own good time.

Suki grew quickly uneasy. Something seemed wrong here, but she couldn't put her finger on it. He looked like a tiger getting ready to pounce. She brushed herself off nervously and tried a light tone. "Next time you close your door, make sure it's locked."

He turned to look at her, capturing her eyes for a long moment as if trying to decide something about her. She looked back at him uncomprehendingly, waiting for the electricity to spark between them again, but he narrowed his eyes and looked away before it could happen. Then he began opening all the drawers, looking obsessively for something that obviously wasn't there.

"What's wrong?" she asked anxiously. "What are you looking for? You're acting as though you were robbed or something." She tried to make it sound like a joke, but her words stopped him cold.

"Am I?" He examined her again, his eyes moving slowly and deliberately over her entire body until she wanted to blush. "Interesting." She could make no sense of this remark, and he began to parade around the room, examining everything from newspapers and magazines to a set of airline tickets sitting on the marble coffee table. Suki looked over his shoulder and noted the destination.

"Rio," she said, surprised. "From Colorado to Brazil—that's some itinerary. What are you doing, traveling around the world?"

"Someone is," he said tersely.

"Someone?" Suki gave him a keen sidelong glance and came to a sinking conclusion. "This isn't your room, is it?"

"Brilliant deduction, Watson."

"Okayyy," she sang under her breath, trying to be cool. "What's going on here?"

"I was hoping you could tell me," he said stonily. "After all, you're the one making the switch, remember? Or should I have said the pickup?" He took a step toward her, and she took an involuntary step back.

"Pickup?" She began to feel panicky. "What are you talking about?" She looked frantically around until she spied the telephone. She'd have to either call the house detective or make a mad dash for the double-locked door.

"You know what pickup," he said, his eyes flashing. "Don't play dumb with me. I'm on to you, Ms.—" He stopped impatiently. "What's your name, anyway? And tell me your real name. I'll find it out sooner or later."

Suki lifted her chin and spoke with quiet dignity. "My name is Suki Lavette, and that's the only name I've got. You seem to be accusing me of something, but I can assure you that your suspicions, whatever prompted them, are completely ill-founded."

"Lovely," he said softly. "An Oscar-winning speech if I ever heard one." He let out a long sigh.

"And the artist's disguise is good, but it's not fooling me, so you can knock it off." His eyes met hers, and they looked almost sad. "I had to admit, though, you had me going for a while. That flustered, dewy-eyed look. The pretty confusion. The way you walk, like a dancer about to twirl into the air." He sighed. "Luchek certainly picked an accomplice beautiful enough to divert my attention." His expression hardened almost against his will. "Yes, you're a sexy little package, Ms. Suki Lavette, but I'm not buying it. The game's up."

"Game?" Suki asked, stalling, taking another step back. "What game?" She began to wonder if she was in any real danger. Probably the best thing to do was to get out of here as quickly as possible.

He refused to explain anything more, but his face was granitelike as he gestured grandly toward the adjoining bedroom. "Let's check in the other room, shall we?" he asked sardonically.

Suki was suddenly angry. This whole scene was becoming insulting. She swept past him into the next room and looked around with an injured air. "I really don't know what you're talking about Mr.—whoever you are," she said pointedly. "But I'm willing to humor you for a while just to prove that I really don't know what you're talking about."

"I'm talking about the old suitcase switch," he said. "Let's face it, why would anyone really buy a piece of luggage as ridiculous as this?" He reached into the closet and triumphantly held up another piece of luggage with an Egyptian design on it. "Aha!"

"My suitcase!" she cried. "Give me that."

He marched her back into the sitting room, placing the suitcase next to the other one and watching her with the same intent gaze. "The question is," he said softly, "which one has the two million dollars in it?"

Suki froze. "Two . . . million . . . dollars?" She pointed down at the suitcase she had carried in. "You aren't going to tell me that there are two million bucks stashed in there, are you?"

"I'm not sure," he said coolly, ignoring her amazement. "It could be in your bag, now, couldn't it?" He pondered that for a moment. "It really depends on whether you're dropping off the money or picking it up." He looked at her curiously, weighing the question.

Suki decided that she'd had enough. A conversation about two million dollars was way out of her league. This was something for the police to handle. "At the moment," she announced, "I'm leaving." She started to reach for her bag, but his hand grabbed hers before she even touched the handle.

Anger flared inside her, momentarily replacing her panic. "Let go of me immediately or I'll—"

"Or you'll what?" He sounded almost baiting, as if he would be amused by what she might try. He pulled her closer, his hands gripping her shoulders.

"I'm warning you," she said.

"You're very tense," he said ironically, his hands still holding her shoulders. "That isn't the direct result of a guilty conscience, is it?"

Suki trembled as his face came near hers. "Who are you, anyway?"

"I'm a detective," he answered. "And right now you're a prime suspect in a very serious crime." He gave her a small, mocking smile. "And you're still tense."

"You're making me that way."

He considered, as if reluctant to press her. "Listen, Suki. You're a nice girl, I can see that." He shook his head. "How did you ever get mixed up in a scheme like this, anyway?" He actually sounded concerned. "You needed the money so badly? Are you the old cliché of the starving artist?"

"I beg your pardon," she retorted. "I happen to be on the brink of success. This tour, which I'm just finishing here, should bring me a lot of attention."

"Then I don't get it," he said, genuinely puzzled. His face softened, and his grip slackened somewhat. "Look, Suki," he said earnestly, his eyes warming her like rays of the sun. "I like you, I really do."

"Then kindly let go of me."

"If I do, will you promise not to run away?"

She looked into his eyes. They were clear and in total control. Obviously, there was some terrible misunderstanding going on here. She had to believe it would get cleared up. All she had to do was tell the truth. "Okay," she said slowly, "I promise."

True to his word, he gently released her, allowing a momentary feeling of truce to pass between them. Suki swallowed nervously. Whoever or whatever he was, he was connected to something very serious. And he was very, very sure of himself. Not only was he capable of bending any situation to his will, he was devastatingly attractive as well. She would have to be extremely careful. She slipped backward, moving away from him.

"I still can't figure you out," he said, noting her

discomfort. "I'm usually an excellent judge of character."

"What's wrong with my character?"

His eyes swept boldly over her petite figure, assessing her. "Nothing. That's what I can't figure out."

"You're not making any sense."

"I'm also not making any headway." His eyes fell back on the two identical suitcases. "So which one has the money?" he mused aloud. "Is it bag number one or bag number two?"

She took this opportunity to move closer to the phone. The man was uncanny, and she wasn't about to take any more chances with him.

"I say it's in your bag." He reached over and flipped open the clasps, deliberately dumping the contents onto the bed.

"Hey, what are you doing?" she cried. "Are you crazy?"

He quickly riffled through her belongings, glaring at her quizzically as he unearthed a purple spiked wig, a pair of Mickey Mouse suspenders, two photographs of Paul Newman, and a large plastic pumpkin.

"I use those things in my work," she said faintly, grabbing her repair kit before it crashed to the floor.

Finally, he threw his arms up in frustration. "It's not here," he muttered savagely.

"Thanks a lot," she said, stepping forward to reclaim her possessions. "Now I'll have to repack all this stuff."

As she began throwing her belongings back into the suitcase, he contemplated the other one. "Then this one must have the money in it. I know I'm right." He looked at Suki. "Very clever. You carry the money, and I end up following Luchek. Not that I wouldn't much prefer to follow you, but business is business." He tried the latches on the second case, but they were locked. "My trusty bobby pin should do the trick," he said.

He began working expertly on the latches, but Suki was too busy repacking to notice. "I don't want to know anything about this," she fumed. "For all I know, *you're* a thief, and you're using me as some kind of patsy. Now, unless you're going to arrest me, I'd like to get out of here and leave you to solve your own problems."

He looked up at her after easily unlocking the latches, and, saying nothing, reached down and scooped up a black-lace bra that had fallen onto the floor. "Here," he said mildly, a twinkle stealing into his deadpan expression. "You forgot this." He held it up and examined it, one eyebrow raised. "Hmmm, not bad."

"Give me that," she snapped, grabbing it out of his hand. She stuffed it inside the suitcase and tried to close the clasp, but the jumbled contents gave her too much difficulty. She had no recourse but to turn to him. "Would you mind giving me a hand?" she asked stiffly.

He took the suitcase obligingly and put it on the floor. By applying all his weight on it, he managed to get the first latch shut.

Suki wasted no time. While he struggled to close the second one, she raced for the door, and would have made it if she hadn't lost her balance. She had the door halfway open before he slammed it back shut.

"Oh, no, you don't." He stood with his body blocking the door. "And you promised me."

"I had my fingers crossed."

"Now, look, I want some answers, and I want them now."

Suki was in a panic. "Let me go or I'll scream."

"Go right ahead." He smiled, challenging her with steely confidence. "No one will hear you."

She opened her mouth, but before she could let out a good, healthy scream, he leaned forward and covered her lips with his.

- 2 -

THEY STOOD TOGETHER INCONGRUOUSLY for a long moment, poised at the beginning of a kiss that waited for her approval. She was too stunned to know what to do. It was clear he didn't intend to hurt her or to force her to do anything she didn't want to do. If she had any sense, she should wriggle out of his grasp and run out the door. But a tiny, crazy voice inside of her told her that she would have been perfectly delighted to kiss this magnetic man under different circumstances. His lips were warm and inviting, promising an untold sweetness if she surrendered. Sheer instinct told her not to move, not to do anything, and it worked.

He lifted his mouth from hers after a long while, and they looked at each other oddly, two people who now shared a secret: They had been on the brink of a lovely intimacy that had been put on hold.

"Don't scream," he said softly.

"I wasn't planning to." This wasn't quite true, but apparently he bought it.

"Good." He flashed her a quick smile. "Then you trust me?"

"No."

"No?" He actually looked disappointed.

"Well, what do you expect?" she asked impatiently.

"I expect you to cooperate."

"With you? Forget it." Again, she opened her mouth to scream, and this time he reacted even more quickly, opening his mouth to capture hers more fully before he claimed it. He kissed her in earnest this time, holding her tightly and seeking her tongue with his. She stared at him wild-eyed, surprised to notice that his eyes were closed and that he was truly enjoying this impromptu kiss. The effect of his arousal stole into her, unwilling though she was to respond. He felt strong and sure and utterly masculine, he smelled of a piney after shave, and he had a beguiling cinnamon taste. Everything about him was hopelessly seductive, and Suki felt her own eyes fluttering to a close as he claimed her.

The kiss ended slowly. "Please just relax," he murmured against her lips. "I swear I won't hurt you." His face was inches from hers as he tried to calm her down. "Please. I can't keep kissing you all day just to keep you quiet."

Her eyes caught sight of the table near the door, where a vase sat just out of reach.

"Promise you won't scream?" he asked lightly, obviously sure that his tactic had worked.

She tried to think clearly, wondering what would

happen if she said no. She could feel his superior strength blocking her, and her senses went into overdrive, totally confused. Everything about him was commanding and masculine, but at this moment he had more than the upper hand. He was after something, and he wasn't going to give up until he found it, whatever it was. He might be quite innocent and harmless, but she had to get away from him before she could make any rational decisions. She eyed him squarely and nodded. "I promise," she said.

"That's better." He beamed.

She looked deeply into his blue eyes, and her heart quickened. He was watching her, not saying a word, trusting that she wouldn't scream.

Slowly, he backed away from her, letting the silence stand as a tacit agreement between them. She knew at that moment that he had never meant her any harm—and yet she wasn't going to take any chances. She had been through enough already. Her hand reached over to the table and groped around, finally settling on the vase.

"There," he said, smiling in reassurance. His eyes caressed her face. "Now, that didn't hurt, did it?"

"No," she said softly, wondering if she really had the nerve to do what she was about to do. "But this will." She brought the vase down on the side of his head, sending him sprawling on the bed. "Owwwwww!" His hand flew to his head, rubbing it furiously as he tried to sit up. Evidently still dazed by the force of the blow, he fell back down again, letting his head clear. "Good God, woman, are you trying to kill me?"

"Maybe," Suki answered with much more bravado than she felt. She brandished the vase over him. "Just don't try any more tricks."

She made a grab for the phone, almost knocking over her sculpture again. After hurriedly steadying it, she found the listing for the hotel detective, and punched the buttons.

"Room 1607!" she cried at once into the phone. "Please come right away! I can't explain now—just hurry!"

She put down the phone, feeling a definite sense of relief, and looked over at the man. "The cavalry is on the way," she informed him.

"Who'd you call?" he bit out. "Your contact? How many of you are there, anyway?"

Suki's anger flared. She had no idea to whom he was referring, and she didn't want to know. She'd had enough of this. "Just don't come any closer, or I'll clobber you again."

"Of that I have no doubt." He tried to sit up, failed, and continued rubbing his sore head. The still-unopened suitcase sat next to him on the floor, and he reached down and patted it as if it were a dog. "Easy come, easy go," he moaned. "I hope you'll be very happy spending it."

Suki watched him carefully, still wary but in full control. "For your information," she said icily, "I have no need to steal anyone's money. I happen to be a working artist." She gestured grandly at her gun-toting sculpture.

He laughed, completely spoiling her regal attitude. "You mean you actually expect me to believe that there are people out there dumb enough to buy that—" He began pointing at her sculpture, but stopped when he saw her eyes flare up. "Uh, what I mean is . . ." He looked at her apologetically, and made a desperate attempt to change the subject. "So, you're supposedly here for a showing, is that the idea?"

"You didn't believe a word I said, did you?"

The sardonic smile returned. "And you don't believe me."

Suki stared at him rudely. "I don't even know who you *are*."

His eyes widened suddenly. "Donald Luchek!" he stated.

She sighed. "So now you claim you *are* Luchek. I wish you'd make up your mind."

"Not me," he said, looking in back of her. "Him."

Suki wheeled around and saw a man in a black-leather jacket and dark sunglasses standing in the doorway, silently turning the lock. In his right hand was a gun.

"Oh, my God!" she screamed.

The newcomer, presumably the real Donald Luchek, smiled icily at Suki, and the smile broadened when he saw the two suitcases. "Well, well, what do we have here? My money, I presume?"

Suki prayed silently, finally finding her voice. "Uh, I took your suitcase by accident at the airport."

"I see. And now you're returning it."

"That's right," Suki confirmed quickly. "And now that I have, I think I'll be going, if you don't mind." She edged over to the door, but Luchek raised the gun at her, all pretense of cordiality abruptly dropped.

"But I do mind," he said in a low, smooth voice. "I'd appreciate it if you'd both put your hands up over your heads." Keeping the gun trained on them, he walked over to where Suki's suitcase sat on the bed next to the alleged detective.

Too shocked and frightened to argue, Suki did as he said. "I don't believe this is happening to me," she said, closing her eyes for a fraction of a second as if to order the whole scene away.

The handsome stranger on the bed remained as he was, refusing to do as their sinister captor demanded. Suki's heart lurched as she saw Luchek's face darken.

"I said hands on top of your head, buddy."

"The name's Colman," he said without moving. "Fletcher Colman."

Luchek's manner grew more intense. "Hands up, Mr. Colman—or would you like me to use this gun?" His voice was still low and controlled, but there was no mistaking the menace in it.

"Do as he says," Suki pleaded.

"Why should I?" Fletcher smiled coolly at Luchek and gestured at the corner next to the door. "Officer Smith over there has you covered."

Luchek laughed. "You don't really think I'd fall for an old trick like that, do you? What kind of a fool do you take me for?"

"A first-class one, Luchek. Officer, arrest this man."

Suki nearly died at his nonchalance as he actually lay back on the bed, lacing his hands behind his head.

Luchek turned carefully around. When he saw Suki's policeman leveling a gun at him, his eyes widened in astonishment. A second later, he dropped the gun and was raising his hands in defeat.

Suki instinctively rushed for the gun and aimed it

at Luchek. She had never held a gun before, but despite her private doubt that she could actually figure out how to fire it, it looked impressively threatening in her hands.

"Okay, hands up, mister," she ordered sternly. Luchek complied at once, and she felt a thrill of confidence.

Fletcher suddenly broke into a huge grin. He pointed at the sculpture. "You were fooled by a mannequin."

Luchek's face dropped. "A mannequin!"

"It's a sculpture," Suki corrected him.

"And a darn good one at that," Fletcher added proudly, still rubbing his head but obviously pleased. "You really are an artist."

"That's right, I am. Now get your hands up, too, buster." She raised the gun higher and pointed it right at him.

Fletcher looked hurt, as if she had just insulted him. "I beg your pardon. Surely you can't mean that I—"

"Especially you," she said. The gun was heavier than she had expected, and she used both hands to steady it.

"I really don't see why you think *I* would be a threat to you," Fletcher insisted.

"Just don't move, buster," Suki threatened.

Luchek was staring dumb struck at the sculpture. "It looks so, so—"

"Real," Fletcher filled in.

"Yeah," Luchek said, shaking his head in wonder. Quickly gathering his composure, he turned back to Suki, who was still pointing the gun. "Careful, young lady, it's cocked." He turned to Fletcher, who was still camped out on the bed. "Tell her to be careful," he growled.

"Why bother? She's going to have to kill us sooner or later."

"What?" Suki couldn't believe her ears. "You're crazy."

"Am I?" The brilliant lake-blue eyes regarded her with an utter lack of fear that unnerved her. "How else do you plan to get away with the money?"

"What are you talking about? I don't want the money. All I want is my suitcase and my sanity, both of which you two have somehow managed to take from me. Good Lord," she complained aloud, "I can't believe this is happening to me."

Suddenly, there was a knock at the door. They all froze.

"Detective Spalding here. Open up."

"Oh, thank goodness," Suki breathed.

Fletcher turned to her, surprised. "You really did call the hotel detective?"

She smiled and nodded, her eyes on the door. "Of course I did." She called hastily to the detective outside, "In here! They tried to kill me."

"She's got a gun," Luchek yelled. "Careful, Officer."

"Wait a minute, I'm the good guy—he's the crook!" Suki shouted.

"Don't believe her, Detective," Luchek shouted. "This is my room. They tried to rob me."

The detective was adamant. "Open up! Now! Or I'll break it down."

Holding the gun higher, Suki backed up toward the door and felt around until her hand found the knob.

The detective spoke again. "I'm warning you in there. You'd better open that door this instant."

Her hand fumbled at the door as she struggled to hold on to the gun, but it was too late. In a second, the house detective crashed through the door against her, sending her careening right at Fletcher. She crashed into him and he grabbed her, preventing her from falling.

"I do wish you'd be more careful," he muttered.

"Well, I'm sorry," she said, dropping the gun.

Luchek scooped up the gun along with the suitcase full of money and ran past Spalding, knocking against the sculpture. The inert policeman fell against the house detective, almost knocking him down.

"He's getting away!" Suki yelled.

Fletcher pushed Suki aside and made a mad dash after him, but Suki blocked his way, almost tripping him.

"Where do you think you're going?" she asked with new authority, suddenly more confident now that Luchek was gone and Spalding had arrived.

He looked at her for a split second, his keen eyes boring into hers. "After Luchek and all that money. You wouldn't mind getting out of my way, would you?"

"Yes, I would mind," she retorted, matching his gaze coolly. He laughed softly and let his eyes roam provocatively over her face before he turned and chased after Luchek, leaving her to stare after his lithe, retreating form.

"I can't believe so much could happen to a person in one day!" Suki exclaimed, her hands waving wildly around her animated face. "Mixing up luggage is one thing—that happens, okay, but to be *shot* at—"

"No one shot anyone, Ms. Lavette," Detective Spalding broke in, depositing Suki's luggage on her bed in her hotel room. He was a portly man, clearly unused to perilous scenes in this resort town. He tried to make a hasty exit, but she stopped him.

"Well, what about the gun?"

Spalding took a deep breath. "I didn't see any gun. And as far as that Detective Tollman is concerned—"

"Colman," Suki corrected sternly. Couldn't the man get his facts straight? "Fletcher Colman."

Spalding shrugged. "Whatever. Whoever he is, I never heard of him."

Suki could sense that he wanted out of this entire situation, and she tried to glean the last bits of information from him before he took off. "Isn't he registered at this hotel?"

"Nope," Spalding answered smugly. "Now, if you don't mind, I've got a seventy-eight-year-old lady in 402 with a claim about a peeping tom that needs immediate attention."

He departed, leaving a disgruntled Suki very much alone in her room. "He probably thinks I made the whole thing up," she mumbled to herself after locking and double-locking the door and adding the chain for good measure. "Crazy, that's what it is. Just one of those extremely bad days. One of those extremely awful very bad days." Desperate for reassurance, she began an impromptu version of a song. "Just one of those days," she warbled tunelessly. Her voice fell off in defeat as she looked dejectedly at her favorite sculpture, the broken piece lying on the floor beside it. She picked up the repair kit, but put it down with a sigh.

"What I really need now is a hot bubble bath, some decent wine, and some fruit and cheese. Then I should jump right into bed with a good book."

That got her into motion. She picked up the phone and dialed room service. "This is Suki Lavette in Room 1313." She shuddered at the implications of that number before continuing. "Would you please send up a bottle of white wine, pouilly-fuissé if you have it, some fresh strawberries, Norwegian crackers, and fontina cheese. Oh, and no hurry. I'd like to take a bath first."

With renewed confidence, she went over to her suitcase, flipped the latches, and threw the lid back.

The shock almost choked her. "Oh, my God."

Instead of her belongings, which she had tossed pell-mell into her suitcase after Fletcher Colman dumped them out out, she found it packed to the gills with stacks of money.

She drew a long, uneven breath and let it out shakily. Then she closed her eyes against the incredible sight as if to will it away. She opened her eyes a crack and peeked at it again.

It was still there.

As she stared at it in disbelief, her heart began to gallop. "Maybe it's just a hallucination. That's it," Suki tried to convince herself. "It's just a figment of an overworked imagination. If I touch it, it will disappear."

She reached down and picked up a stack of twenties no thicker than an inch, then flipped through it like a deck of cards. "There must be close to ten thousand dollars in this stack," she murmured reverently to herself. "So that's how they can fit two million dollars into a suitcase."

Her next rational thought was to call Spalding. She placed the wad of money by the phone, picked up the receiver, and began dialing. *"Two . . . million . . . dollars,"* she gasped, the words coming out in a tiny squeak. She played rhythmically with the stack of twenties as the phone continued ringing without an answer. Spalding was probably still handling that old lady and her peeping tom, she figured.

Suddenly, there was a knock at the door. Suki froze.

"Hello in there, it's me." The voice was Fletcher Colman's. "Suki?"

"Oh, no." Hanging up the phone, she whipped around and stared at the suitcase full of money. "Just a minute!" she called out nervously. "I—I'm not dressed."

She ran over and banged the suitcase shut, wondering what to do with it. Hide it, she thought to herself, and quickly dragged it off the bed, letting it land on the floor with a thud.

"Suki? Are you all right?"

"Yes, I'll be right there." She pushed the suitcase under the dresser, composed herself quickly, and was about to head for the door when she spotted the stack of twenties by the phone.

"Oh, Lord."

"Suki? Are you all right?"

"Yes," she blurted out. "I'm just buttoning up." Snatching the money, she conveniently shoved it into her purse and tossed it on the bed.

Out of breath, she unlocked the door, leaving the

chain attached. The door opened six inches, and Fletcher stared at her through the crack.

"Hello again," he said cheerfully. His eyes swept over her appreciatively, as if he were calling to pick her up for an evening out. She couldn't believe his insouciance.

"You should be arrested, do you know that?" she demanded, hoping to squelch the confident masculine interest on his face.

"Yes, well, I'm not so sure you shouldn't be arrested also, but let's not quibble over details." He looked her over quizzically before continuing. "In any case, I came by to apologize." He didn't sound sorry at all, and her temper flared.

"Apology accepted. Now go away." She tried to shut the door again, but he held it open with one hand. "Let go of my door, please," she insisted, her heart quickening.

His voice became smooth and authoritative, though he retained his aura of casual charm. "Not until you hear what I have to say."

"Why should I? You almost got me killed."

He indicated the bump on his head with a rueful grin. "And just what do you call what you did to me?"

"Self-defense."

"More like attempted murder."

Suki folded her arms in what she hoped was a dignified manner. She should have known he would be hard to handle. Fletcher Colman wasn't the sort of man you could tell to get lost and expect him to do it. He was going to do exactly what he wanted, and the best she could do was to be aware of his every move. "What happened to the man you were chasing?"

Fletcher shrugged. "I lost him, but he won't get far in this blizzard. The roads are very slippery, and the airport is closed."

"What about me?" Suki asked. "Do you still think I was involved in this little caper?"

He got right to the point. "I had you checked out."

"You *what?*"

"I checked you out," he repeated calmly. "To see if you are who you say you are. It's not hard to do," he said in response to her surprise. "All you need is a name and an address. There's a central computer file that gives entire life stories—for a price, of course."

This was too much. First the man almost got her killed, and then he had the nerve to check *her* out? With space-age machinery?

"And who checked *you* out?" she asked. "How do I know you're who you say you are?"

"Fair enough." He moved away from the door and fished in his pocket, pulling out a business card and handing it to her. "Just call my agency in L.A."

"I think I'll do that," Suki said. "But in the meantime, please go away." She slammed the door shut, and waited a few moments to be sure he had left.

"Phew, that was close." She breathed a sigh of relief, and fingered the card in her hand nervously. "Fletcher Colman, Private Investigator."

She should have called the police first, but curiosity and the need to know if he was on the level won out over practicality.

Dialing direct, she got his voice on an answering machine. The message was clearly not rehearsed in any way, and was supplemented with an occasional aside to a woman whose voice could be heard dimly over some jazzy music that had been playing in the room as Fletcher recorded his speech. "Oh, hello, there. This is Fletcher Colman. I'm out of town on a case at the moment—oh, thanks, love, on the rocks—but please leave a message at the sound of the tone." The faint sound of ice cubes clinking in the background came through the wire. "Please don't hang up," the voice continued, "I'm dying to hear from you." This was followed by sultry feminine laughter. "Oh, dear, I didn't mean that, did I? Well, you all know what I mean. Just leave your name and number after the beep."

The beep sounded promptly, and there was nothing to do but leave a message. "This is Suki Lavette." She pondered for a few seconds and finally settled on three choice words. "Leave—me—alone!"

She hung up with a bang and dialed Spalding again, just as there was another knock at the door.

"I don't believe that man." The knocking persisted as she marched over to the door and opened it in frustration, without thinking. "Listen, Colman, I told you to go away already, and I meant—"

She never finished the sentence. The words died in her throat as she stared at Luchek's gun, only inches from her nose.

"Remove the chain, please," he said with menacing patience, obviously aware that he had her where he wanted her. "And do it quickly."

Suki fished around frantically for the end of the chain, and tried to remove it without taking her eyes from the gun.

"Hurry up, please." His voice was as cold as death.

Suki couldn't believe her own stupidity. How

could she have opened the door without looking? But it was too late now. Luchek stepped inside, forcing her backward as he closed the door behind him. He backed her all the way into the corner before he took his eyes off her, letting them sweep over the room. It didn't take long for them to settle on the suitcase, partially visible under the dresser. He lifted the case and threw it on the bed, opened it quickly, and smiled in glorious satisfaction as he regarded the incredible amount of money inside.

Suki said absolutely nothing, afraid that any gesture, any word, would rub him the wrong way.

"Excellent," he said with a grim little laugh. He turned to her, and she froze. "Now, why don't you just have a seat." He gestured to the reclining chair by the phone.

She didn't budge, and he gave her a chilling smile. "Make yourself comfortable."

Suki had no choice but to do as he said, and five unpleasant minutes later she found herself completely bound and gagged. Luchek picked up the suitcase full of money and waved good-bye.

"Good day, young lady, thanks a million." He laughed as the door slammed shut, and Suki was left alone in her room, unable to move and waiting for someone—anyone—to discover her plight.

She didn't have to wait long. A minute later, there was another knock at the door, and her heart leaped with hope as she remembered the food she had ordered.

"It's me again," Fletcher's voice called in. "Come on, open up, I know you're there . . . Suki?" He tried the door, but it was locked.

"MMMMMMM! MMMMMMM!" was all she

could yell, but she kept yelling it in the hope that he would catch on. "MMMMMMM!"

"Suki?" Apparently, he couldn't hear her at all. "Open up."

She tried again, but it was useless. He couldn't hear her. Terrific, she thought. She'd probably remain like this for days!

Then she heard a tiny scraping sound, and when she looked at the door, she saw that the lock was turning. A moment later, Fletcher stood triumphantly inside, holding up a hairpin in one hand and her suitcase in the other.

"Hi," he said, eyeing her dubiously. "Mind if I come in?"

- 3 -

FLETCHER SHOOK HIS HEAD CRITICALLY. "You certainly do get into trouble a lot, don't you?"

She tried to glare at him. "Mmmmmmm," was all she could say.

He shook his head again. "You don't have to explain, I understand everything." He put her suitcase down. "I found this lying in a snowdrift in the parking lot. Obviously, in his haste, Luchek grabbed the wrong bag." He continued shaking his head at her. "I rushed up here the second I found it, but it looks like I missed Luchek by seconds, didn't I?"

Suki nodded impatiently, and her eyebrows went up in frustration as she tried to indicate that he should untie her, but he didn't make a move.

"Well, he won't get far," Fletcher said cheerfully. "I cut the wires in his car. Besides, the roads are impassable."

Suki was glad to hear that, but she would be even more glad if he would release her. Her eyes pleaded silently, but Fletcher ignored her.

"Do you know what your problem is, Suki?" he asked with friendly interest.

She gazed at him murderously.

"You don't trust anyone. And you're too impatient."

"Mmmmmmm." Her gaze turned urgent. He was actually going to lecture her at a time like this. She couldn't believe him. And on the subject of trust! Look who's talking, she wanted to shout. But she couldn't say anything, and he continued as casually as if she were hanging willingly onto every word.

"Now don't try to deny it."

Another knock at the door stopped him cold.

"Room service," a young man called in.

"Room service?" He smiled at Suki. "How thoughtful of you."

He turned his attention momentarily away from her.

"Just leave it by the door," he ordered. "I'm not dressed."

He waited for the bellhop to leave before bringing the tray of food inside.

All Suki could do was watch furiously as Fletcher put the tray on the bed and stretched out alongside it. "Ah, an excellent wine," he commented, pouring some pouilly-fuissé deftly into a glass. He lifted it toward her in a toast. "To your health." He took a sip and smiled. "Mmm, dry and full-bodied. Delightful."

Suki's only thoughts were how she was going to

bash his head in with the bottle once she got out of that chair.

"Now, I'm going to say what I have to say, and you have no choice but to listen. Face it, Suki, you're a captive audience." He smiled broadly, as if the idea amused him immensely. Suki struggled valiantly, but succeeded only in hiking her dress up to the middle of her thighs.

Fletcher watched this performance with undisguised interest. "You are making this difficult for me, aren't you?" he sighed. She breathed heavily in anger, and he put down his glass. "Oh, very well. If you insist." Reaching over to hold the hem of her skirt, he pulled it down slowly, letting his hand graze the length of her slender, well-toned thigh. "Better?" He patted her knee solicitously. "I thought so."

Letting his hand remain intimately on her knee, he picked up his glass with the other hand and went on. "I'm going to tell you the truth," he said seriously. "But you can't breathe a word of what I'm saying to anyone. Do you promise?"

Suki gritted her teeth and nodded. The effect of his hand was amazingly intense. A pool of heat seemed to emanate from it, spreading rapidly up her leg. There was nothing she could do about it, but maybe his words would distract her. She looked at him expectantly, ready to listen.

"Good." He ate a strawberry with leisurely relish. "I'm working very discreetly on this case," he began, eyeing her pointedly. "No one can know that this two million dollars was stolen."

"Hmmm?"

"Have patience, I'll explain. Remember that big,

sold-out rock festival last weekend down in San Diego? It was in all the papers."

Suki nodded. She did remember.

"Good. Well, Luchek was handling the ticket sales at the gate. Seems he conveniently forgot to make any bank deposits. He disappeared, leaving the producer of the concert with about one and a half million dollars' worth of unpaid bills."

He waited for Suki to digest this, taking the opportunity to sip more wine.

"If anyone finds out that the money was stolen, my client will never again be trusted in the music industry to produce another concert. As it is, he has less than three weeks before his creditors start to get suspicious."

The phone rang, making Suki jump, but Fletcher got up and answered it, mercifully releasing her knee.

"Hello, Suki Lavette's room." Unfortunately, his hand now fell lightly on her shoulder, massaging it gently as if to reassure her. "That's great news, I'll tell her." After hanging up, he dropped back down on the bed again. "They just delivered your sculptures," he announced. "I'm supposed to tell you to go downstairs in fifteen minutes and start setting up the exhibit."

"Mmmmmmm!" Suki gestured at her bonds with darts shooting from her eyes.

"Oh, don't worry, I'm going to untie you. I just want you to know where we stand." He finished off his glass of wine and ate a piece of cheese. "As far as I'm concerned, you're still suspect. That Little Miss Innocent routine back in Luchek's room wasn't totally convincing, I'm afraid. You handled that gun just a little too awkwardly. No one can be that clumsy, especially with a thirty-two Beretta. It's made so that even a woman can shoot it."

She gave him the iciest stare she could muster.

He looked up at her pleasantly, as though she had just reminded him of something else. "Oh, yes, I was just coming to that." Putting down the empty glass of wine, he went over and put his hands gently on her shoulders.

"As far as that coincidence of just happening to have the same ridiculous-looking luggage as Mr. Luchek—" He paused and gazed into her eyes.

Suki waited for him to finish, but she could see that it didn't matter. He was not convinced of her innocence, and he wouldn't be until he could prove it himself. She began to despair of ever getting out of that chair, when he bent down and began untying her bonds. He freed her feet first, deliberately leaving the gag on, but she submitted willingly, knowing that any moment she would be able to defend herself. But untying her hands was another matter. Luchek had tied them not only to each other, but also to the back of the carved chair. The only way for Fletcher to reach them was to slide his hands around her waist.

This took some time, during which his face was only inches from hers and her breasts were crushed perilously against his chest. He didn't say a word, but she was positive that he was as aware of this as she was.

When at last her hands were free, she lifted them herself and hastily untied the gag, breathing a huge sigh of relief.

Fletcher smiled winsomely. "There you are, no harm done, right?"

She leaped out of the chair and stretched, trying to look unfazed, but her effort was spoiled by her obvious and boundless relief.

"Come on," he said. "It wasn't that bad. You just had a mild shock, that's all. You'll get used to these minor inconveniences if you continue to dabble with men like Luchek." He poured her a glass of wine. "Luckily for you, I showed up to help."

Suki found her voice and exploded. "Just stay away from me, do you understand? I don't need your 'help'. You've gotten me into enough trouble already."

"But my dear Ms. Lavette, that's where you're wrong. If it weren't for me, you'd be in even bigger trouble than you already are." He smiled mischievously, and his eyes twinkled, as if he knew a secret and wasn't telling her. "You've got to trust someone, Suki, and you're making a big mistake if you don't pick me." His voice had turned husky, and he advanced toward her, studying her face with its rapidly changing series of emotions.

In a moment, he was standing directly in front of her, his eyes enveloping her face, and all rational thought went out of her as she stood under his spell.

"You just need a little convincing," he murmured, and before she knew what was happening, he had stepped forward again and pressed his lips softly to hers.

Suki was too surprised to do anything but stand there. And besides, the brief kiss was turning into a much longer, more complex exchange, tinged with an unearthly sweetness that hinted at abundant sensuality. This time he wasn't trying to silence her, and there was nothing to prevent her from stopping him.

And yet she didn't. She couldn't. Despite all his teasing, all the doubts between them, and all the scares she had had, there was something gloriously inevitable about standing here in Fletcher's arms, surrendering to this most intoxicating kiss. Whatever else happened, she knew that this was something they had to pursue, a question that had to be answered. It made no sense at all. She should be furious with him, of course, but he was probably right. She did need him, at least for the moment, and when he touched her like this, she had no defenses left at all.

They clung together feverishly, searching for and finding a rhythm that united them on a single plane. A small sigh of pleasure escaped first from her and then from him, sealing the unspoken pact they had made. When at last the kiss broke, Suki looked up dreamily into Fletcher's eyes, expecting to see the same sense of wonder she knew was shining in hers.

Instead, she saw a glimmer of smugness, a self-satisfied smirk that told her he had her exactly where he wanted her. Instantly, her temper flared. "Just—don't do me any favors," Suki said huffily. "I can take care of myself."

"No, you can't," Fletcher retorted calmly. "And like it or not, I'm going to have to keep an eye on you until this is over." He smiled. "I don't know about you, but I think I'm going to enjoy watching you . . . a lot."

"But why?" she demanded, startled. "I can't see how you can still suspect me. Not after you found me like this."

"You're not officially under suspicion," he said, walking over to refill his wineglass. His casualness was unnerving. He returned to her, handed her her untasted wine, and tipped his glass against hers before taking a sip. "But from this moment on, you're under my care, understand?"

Suki wasn't convinced. "Sounds more like you're arresting me," she ventured.

"Oh, no," he said, brandishing the wineglass under her nose and throwing her a masculine look of unmistakable sexual invitation. "This is a purely protective custody."

"I don't need protective custody," Suki protested for the hundredth time as, later that evening, she finished the final repairs on her policeman statue's bottom. Fletcher ignored her outburst as he lifted the last sculpture from its crate. Suki hadn't asked him to join her, but he had appeared cheerfully as if he had been scheduled to come and was of vital importance to her work. "What I do need is a good night's sleep."

"And I'll make sure you get it," Fletcher said as he carefully lowered the statue to the floor. "But stop your useless protesting. Besides, who are you kidding? You need me here."

He was right, Suki conceded to herself. It would have been nerve-racking to work alone after such a trying day. Besides, Fletcher had unpacked every sculpture, a chore Suki was glad to relinquish.

She looked around the exhibit hall, checking to make sure everything was in its proper place. Standing at odd angles all over the Jefferson Room were plastic sculptures of people from all walks of life. There was a group of tourists wearing Hawaiian shirts and binoculars, a sunbather, a boxer, a soldier, kids eating melting ice cream, and a man walking a dog on a leash. All of them looked uncannily real.

"'Anticipation of a Kiss,'" Fletcher said aloud as he read the label on the last statue. He pulled off the protective plastic tarp to reveal two figures standing in each other's arms, their faces only inches apart. "That's what it is, all right." He studied this statue judiciously, more than he had studied any of the others, and Suki hid a nervous smile.

"I tried to capture the moment right before," Suki explained hastily as she came over and adjusted the sculpture into position. She really didn't want to talk to Fletcher about kissing. She had the feeling that if she did, a demonstration would quickly follow.

"The moment before can be a long time," Fletcher remarked with interest, still examining the sculpture. "It can be just as exciting as the kiss itself, when it finally comes. Is that what you had in mind?"

"Uh—yes. I guess so." There was a momentary pause between them that was charged with electricity. Suki avoided looking at him, knowing all too well that he was looking at her.

"Of course, there are many different kinds of kisses," Fletcher continued. By now, Suki was sure he was trying to embarrass her, and she was determined not to let him throw her.

"That's true," she allowed carefully.

"For example, there's the chaste, awkward kiss of a teenager, which I don't think this is," he said, examining the statue once more. "This looks more like two people who have made love before and know exactly what's going to happen. This kiss will probably start out gently but will quickly turn passionate. No doubt with a good deal of French kissing toward the end." He turned to her with a clinical air. "I hope you weren't planning on doing a sculpture of *that*. French kissing is the sort of thing that's delightful to do, but not always so delightful to look at."

Suki could not believe his outrageous statements, but she decided to play along. If he thought she couldn't match his maddening coolness, he was wrong. "Oh, I don't know," she said calmly, "I think French kissing is actually rather delicate. If initiated too quickly, of course, it can be—well, rather gauche—but when it's done properly, it takes on a special quality all its own. Of course," she added, "I wasn't referring to how it *looks*. To tell you the truth, I have no idea how it looks. I never really thought of it that way." Pleased with her train of thought, she faced him with an air of challenge. "Why? Are you in the habit of watching couples French-kiss?"

He gave her an amused smirk. "No, not really, although I'm not fond of twenty-foot lips grinding at each other across a movie screen. I was hoping you wouldn't reproduce anything along those lines."

This conversation, which she had hoped to control, was heading in exactly the wrong direction. "I—I'll keep your comments in mind," she said, busying herself with the statue again. Quickly changing the subject, she added, "It must be after midnight."

"Past my bedtime," he agreed heartily. "Shall we?"

Once again, there was an unbearable silence between them. Suki floundered. "Uh—*you* shall," she distinguished. "And I shall, too—in my room." She marched over and turned out the lights, hoping to effectively end the evening once and for all.

But her action had exactly the opposite effect.

Now the only source of illumination came from under the doorway that led to the hotel lobby. Cast into sudden darkness, the room became an eerie collection of shadows. Suddenly, the conversation, which had felt like a roller coaster before, seemed perfectly natural. Suddenly, anything was possible amid this collection of illusion and shadow.

Fletcher was leaning against the wall, and he blinked rapidly. "Suki? Where are you?"

"Right in front of you. Just walk over here."

"That's easier said than done." He laughed. "Everything in here looks so real, I can't tell you from the sculptures."

"Is that a compliment?" she asked breathlessly, watching him slink through the inert figures around them. He moved with a natural grace, the taut, masculine lines of his body tantalizingly evident in silhouette.

He laughed. "Just move a little so I can find you. Wave your arms or something."

She laughed as he reached out and grabbed the sculpture of the sunbather, mistaking it for her. "My God, this is spooky," he said. "It looks so much like you."

"That's because I used myself to make the mold." She walked over and reached for him, but touched the sculpture of the boxer instead.

"I saw that," he said at once. "You're just as lost as I am."

She whirled around, trying to find him, but he was too well camouflaged. "Fletcher?" she called uncertainly. "Where are you? Fletcher?"

"I'm right behind you." His arms came around her suddenly, and he held her against his long, lean form. A shock of recognition passed through her, shot with the beginnings of a deep desire.

"'Anticipation of a Kiss,'" he murmured, echoing her own thoughts. "We'd make a great exhibit. Do you think anyone could tell us from the real thing?"

She shuddered slightly from the anticipation, and he held her tighter. "Mmm, your perfume—Obsession, isn't it?"

"How did you know that?" she whispered.

"A good detective has to know a great deal of things."

"Like what?" She knew she was stalling, but she needed time. Everything was snowballing suddenly, as if something between them had been decided and settled now that they were out of danger. Fletcher seemed to take it for granted that he could hold her like this. Even now, his hands were intimately stroking the side of her neck.

Not that she was doing anything to stop him. It seemed perfectly natural to let herself be swept away. This man had come catapulting into her life, and she knew that his impact was irrevocable. She could fairly feel the sparks igniting and growing quietly between them in the shadowy room.

"What did you do, go to detective school or something?" she asked.

"Or something," he answered, dropping a slow, tantalizing flurry of kisses down the side of her smooth face.

She shivered, and his hands found the feminine contours of her hips. "Don't be afraid of me, Suki."

"I'm not afraid," she said at once. "I just don't want to get involved in anything dangerous." Her eyes flickered. "Besides, we're on very shaky ground, remember? You still don't know whether I'm involved in this mess or not." A shadow crossed her face, one of impatience and sadness. It wasn't pleasant being reminded that this dynamic man didn't quite trust her. It made her angry, and yet somehow she sensed that he would sort everything out and learn for himself that she had had nothing to do with it. If Fletcher was good at what he did—and of that she had no doubt—he would come to the truth on his own. She didn't want to be a lady who protested too much, and so there was nothing to do but carry on naturally.

"Don't worry about that," he said softly. "I have to track down clues, and I have to be logical, but that doesn't mean that my instincts don't count as well. And my instincts tell me that you are a very special person. There's no way in a million years you'd get messed up with a character like Luchek. Don't you think I know that?" There was a soulful note in his voice, as if he wanted to forget all about Luchek and just concentrate on her.

"Thank you," she said simply. "I needed to hear you say that."

"It's true."

A feminine instinct took over as she perceived the longing in his tone. He wanted to know her, not just analyze her. "And I'm certainly not afraid of you," she reassured him. It was true. She couldn't possibly be afraid of anyone who looked at her so openly, with such yearning in his eyes. "Perhaps," she continued, gently teasing, "you should be afraid of me. After all, I've caused you an awful lot of trouble already."

"Oh, I *am* afraid of you," he assured her wryly.

"I'm smart enough to know when someone is dangerous, believe me." He paused, his eyes twinkling. "But it's not any physical jeopardy that scares me, Suki. You're simply the most intriguing, baffling, infuriating woman I've ever met."

"Oh. Was that supposed to be a compliment?"

"Yes."

A provocative light danced through her eyes. "But you don't really know anything about me."

"On the contrary." He smiled smugly. "I had you checked out, remember? Your name is Suzuki Lavette, and you were born in Chicago. Your hobbies are skiing, roller-skating, and gourmet cooking. The latter entices me to invite myself over for a dinner one day in your loft on the outskirts of Denver, Colorado. Would you like to hear more?"

Suki was stunned. How could he learn so much in such a short time? "And what about you," she pushed, suddenly aware of her disadvantage. If he was that well informed about her, she had some catching up to do.

"Oh, I'm your basic preppie turned adventurer," he said with the casual shrug of one who is used to proceeding with utmost confidence in any endeavor. Suki found that simple, masculine shrug wildly appealing. "I started out as a criminal lawyer in Boston, but that got pretty dull. My family wanted me to stay on in my uncle Anthony's firm, but it all seemed so predictable. A partnership, then a senior partnership with associates to do all the footwork and summers with the family in Maine . . . I wanted something different, something of my own."

Suki noticed for no reason at all that his chest muscles were clearly evident through his shirt. Suddenly, she wanted to push the pristine fabric aside and explore the hard contours of that chest. But all she said was, "So now you're out catching crooks and murderers."

He smiled. "It isn't always like that. Sometimes it's ridiculously easy, sometimes it's life-threatening, and sometimes it's a lot of painstaking research. But it changes from day to day, and it keeps me on my toes."

"I guess I don't know much about it," she said, returning his smile a bit tremulously. It was true, she didn't, but she liked his spirit. His was no ordinary profession, and if people didn't understand it, she could identify with that. People rarely understood her work, either. But her work was challenging, opening up new doors, and she sensed that his was, too. "All I know is Kojak and Baretta," she added honestly. Her smile took on an impish light. "And you're not much like either of them."

"Aha, so the artist indulges in some mundane American pastimes like television," he noted.

"Hey, I'm normal." They chuckled together, arousal seeping in and intertwining them in its magic. There was no reason for them to be standing this close, but Suki wouldn't have moved for anything in the world, and she was positive that he wouldn't either. "Don't you do anything besides chase crooks and—whatever?" she asked.

"Sure. I go bobsledding."

"*Bob*sledding? You mean like sleigh riding?"

"Not quite. As in toboggan run," he explained dryly. "As in hurtling straight down a track of solid ice on nothing but a piece of flimsy metal. I almost made the American team a few Olympics ago."

"Oh," she said, cowed. She gazed at him boldly, her green eyes wide. "You do like danger, don't you?"

"I like challenge. Whether in a suspect"—his hands lid enticingly down her arms and his eyes followed—"or in a woman."

"Or both," she couldn't help adding. "I seem to fit into both categories, don't I?"

"Only for the moment. We'll get rid of the first, and then we'll concentrate very slowly on the second." His eyes softened, taking in the details of her slender form. "Don't worry, Suki. I'll watch out for you. You're still vulnerable, you know."

Suki frowned, trying to still the fluttering of her heart. "I am? But Luchek has his money. What else could he want?"

Fletcher's face came closer to hers. "You don't know these bastards. This isn't over yet, not by a long shot." His arms tightened around her waist, pulling her closer, and the shock of her breasts pressing against his strong chest assailed them both.

"Are you sure?" she asked, desire obliterating what was left of logic. She barely knew what she was saying anymore, but she felt she had to say something.

"I'm a detective, remember. It's my job to know what people are really thinking. And right now I know you're wondering what it would be like to kiss me again."

There was no point in denying this. It was written in every nuance of her face, every line of her body. Her eyes closed as he lifted her chin, studying her face for a long, grave moment. He drew closer and closer until there was only a breath of space between them. Then their lips touched, charging them both with a jolt of electricity.

But as they were about to savor this private and intensely intimate moment, the door to the exhibit hall opened slowly, casting a long ray of light across the room. Suki's eyes flew open as the recognizable silhouette of a large man carrying a suitcase entered the room. In his other hand was a gun.

"It's Luchek," Fletcher whispered tightly. His mouth was still only inches from hers. "Don't move."

"Fletcher." Suki could hardly talk. She was a jumble of cheated desire and fear. "I'm scared."

"Just . . . don't . . . move."

Luchek shut the door, and they were once more blanketed in darkness. Suki shuddered but remained immobile.

"Good girl." Fletcher's words were barely audible. "Shh, relax and just lean against me for support."

Fear rippled through her, but Fletcher's arms kept her from moving as Luchek passed within feet of them. He moved to a corner of the exhibit hall out of earshot, but also out of sight.

Suki couldn't stand it. "What's he doing?" she asked.

"Shh." Fletcher managed a fleeting smile. "He's probably hiding out in here. Let's hope he won't be here all night. I'm not going to stand like a statue for the next six hours."

They could hear Luchek rustling with something, but it was too dark to see. The quiet rustling went on interminably, until Suki wanted to scream with frustration.

Then Luchek lit a match, sending a tiny glow of light through the darkness. Suki froze as his footsteps approached, stopping once as he dodged one of the sculptures and then continuing. Closer and closer he came, until he was standing only five feet away, right in front of the sunbather. Suki's heart was pounding so hard that she couldn't believe no one else could hear it. She willed herself to remain motionless, staring straight into Fletcher's eyes.

Luchek lit another match, holding it up briefly. Suki's heart almost stopped as she waited for him to recognize them, to touch them, to accuse them.

An unbearable moment passed. Fletcher didn't even tense. Then Luchek let out a deprecating chuckle. "And people call this stuff art?" he muttered.

Suki had to force herself to remain calm and to keep silent as he turned on his heel and strode out of the room.

They could hear him let out one last chuckle before he opened the door and left.

"Phew," Suki breathed, collapsing against Fletcher's chest the moment Luchek was gone. "What was he doing here?"

"Most probably hiding out for a few minutes," Fletcher said as he ran for the door. His entire demeanor had changed. Now he was all business, a steely, determined glint replacing the tenderness that had shone in his eyes only minutes before.

"Hey," Suki called, fumbling after him. "Wait for me."

"No," Fletcher said authoritatively. He strode back to her, his hands gripping her arms. "Listen to me. Go back to your room and lock the door, and don't open it for anyone."

"But—"

"Suki, please. Do as I say." His eyes flickered for one tiny instant, and her heart contracted.

"All right," she whispered. "But when—"

He didn't give her time to finish. In a flash, he was out the door, running after Luchek, and Suki stood alone, trying to still the trembling that had overtaken her.

- 4 -

SUKI SLEPT SURPRISINGLY WELL, considering what she had been through the day before. With daylight came a firm resolve to return to normal. She wanted no more of thieves and suspects and chases. She opened her shade, using her toe to pull the cord, and was introduced to the immense mountain that was flooded with sunlight.

Early-morning skiers had already hit the slopes, and the clear, beautiful sight lifted her spirits, making her eager to rush outside and join them. Perhaps Fletcher would come with her. She wasn't at all sure what would happen between them, but she was glad now that they had been interrupted last night—even by the unsavory Luchek. Everything was happening too swiftly. She wanted a return to a sane, methodical existence, and Fletcher would just have to fit into that plan.

Nevertheless, as she went over to the closet to peruse her clothes, she found herself rejecting a pair of jeans in favor of a new, sleek ski outfit that flattered her figure.

A half hour later, after a luxurious bubble bath, a thorough washing of her thick hair with a lemon rinse, and a careful application of makeup, she swung her purse over her shoulder and headed downstairs for breakfast. She had no idea if she would see Fletcher Colman or not, but she had already decided not to plan her schedule around him.

But when she entered the dining room, there he was, seated comfortably at a curved banquette under a huge picture window showing a panoramic view of the sprawling mountain. He was dressed, as he had been yesterday, in a beautifully tailored suit. As soon as he saw her, he waved vigorously, obviously anxious to see her.

"I've been waiting close to an hour for you," he announced.

Suki laughed, pleased. What kind of man except a very confident one would ever admit to something like that? She sat down next to him rather than across from him, ostensibly to share the view but also because she liked the tingle of anticipation caused by sitting so close to him. Her recent resolve to take it slow with him, so sensible and sane in the safety of her room, took a sudden back seat when she looked at him.

"Beautiful," he remarked.

Suki smiled. "It's the new snow that fell during the night that makes it glimmer like that. Like diamonds strewn over the mountain."

"I wasn't referring to the view."

She tried to summon up a modest blush, but it was difficult. She was too proud of the picture she had strived to make and the knowledge that she had succeeded. Fletcher wasn't fooled.

"I can always tell when a woman has spent hours preparing herself," he said, reaching out to touch her hair. "Your hair looks like a storm of silk, you smell bewitching, your face is alive with anticipation, and everything about you is charged with a special energy, as if something wonderful is about to happen. It's the most powerful kind of beauty a woman can summon—the kind that's lit from within."

This time Suki really did blush. "I—thank you," she stammered. "You're very—observant. Is that from years of being a detective?"

"No, just male instinct," he answered candidly. He gave her a curious smile, one that was genuinely appreciative and yet somehow guarded. It occurred to her that perhaps she could never really know him. He was too adept at concealing his thoughts and at saying whatever was necessary to extract the information he needed. "I like it," he added, leaning back to admire her.

"Well, thanks," she said again, flustered.

Fletcher smiled once more. "Do you deny it? Or do you always look like that?"

There was only one safe answer to that question. "Oh, I always look like this," she assured him blithely. Then she remembered a convenient excuse. "Plus I happen to have a show tonight—or did you forget?"

He gave her an enigmatic little grin. "I didn't forget. I never forget anything. I can't afford to, in my profession." Changing the subject deftly, he added, "What are your plans for the day?"

"Skiing," she answered, "and maybe an afternoon swim in the pool."

Fletcher laughed. "How very touristic of you."

"Maybe," she allowed, "but I need some relaxation after the—events of yesterday. Not to mention the tediousness of this tour. This is the sixth city I've been to, and I'm at the point where I can't tell one from the next."

He absorbed this statement wordlessly, but his keen eyes were watching her the whole time.

Suki sighed elaborately. "Now don't give me that detective look of yours, Fletcher. You know, it's really not your best side."

Fletcher didn't flinch. He leaned forward, studying her so intently that his eyes seemed to harden into glass. "You know, Suki," he said slowly, "up until I met you, I prided myself on always being on top of things, but you've put a chink in my armor. In fact, if I'm ever going to solve this case, I may have to let my guard down entirely with you. And that's never a good idea in my business."

Suki was stung. "What do you mean?" she cried. "After last night I thought—everything was so—" She stopped herself, unwilling to reveal how he had affected her, but he only nodded grimly.

"Exactly," he said. Their eyes met and deadlocked. Suki was seized with an instinct to defend herself—against what, she didn't know—and she realized that something must have happened after he had gone chasing after Luchek. Her heart sank.

"Why don't you tell me what happened last night," she suggested quietly. "Did you ever catch

Luchek? And what about the money? Did you find it?"

"All in good time," Fletcher said, withdrawing sharply, as if satisfied that the subject had finally been brought up but unwilling to jump into it unless he had absolute control over it. "Let's order first." He picked up the menu and examined it, coolly cutting off her questions.

Suki wasn't reassured. "You're not telling me something," she said slowly. "What happened last night?"

He waved the waiter over. "The Belgian waffles are excellent here," he told her.

"Fine," she said dully.

"Two Belgian waffles," he said to the waiter. "And two orange juices, and coffee."

The waiter poured them coffee and left.

"Are you going to tell me about Luchek or not?" Suki asked the moment they were alone. "Did you catch him?"

"I didn't have to. In fact, he caught me."

"What?"

"It was all very simple. After I left you, I followed him downstairs into the bar, where he sat himself down at a table and offered me a seat." He looked at Suki for a reaction, but she said nothing. "We drank cognacs together," Fletcher continued. "Everything was cordial. We spoke like two gentlemen negotiating a simple business transaction. He coolly offered me ten thousand dollars to go away and leave him alone."

"Ten thousand dollars." Suki let the words out too fast.

"Naturally, I laughed in his face," Fletcher explained. "I pride myself on an impeccable reputation, which includes a one-hundred-percent track record." His eyes bored into hers. "I always come up a winner, you see. Haven't disappointed a client yet."

"I see. You always get your man, huh?"

"Something like that," he said.

"Now Luchek must really be afraid of you," she guessed.

"Not in the least. I never saw a more confident man." He paused, as if unsure how much to tell her, but then he continued quickly. "I'm positive he's hidden the money somewhere nearby, and he won't go near it until he's sure I'm far enough away. My guess is he'll wait a couple of weeks or even months before retrieving it. So, for the moment, my best move is to stay as far away from Donald Luchek as I can. I'll give him enough rope and let him hang himself. Unfortunately, I don't have too much time."

Suki was speechless at this revelation, and it was just as well that the waiter brought their waffles while she absorbed the situation. She took an automatic bite of a strawberry, and the sweet, pungent flavor awakened her to the fact that she was very hungry.

"Let's eat a little first," Fletcher advised. "I don't want to say what I'm about to say on an empty stomach."

"Oh, no. There's more?" She looked at him beseechingly, but he merely pointed to her plate.

"Eat," he said.

What started out as a cordial conversation had quickly turned into an unsatisfying mystery. Suki decided to follow his advice and get some nourishment. Fletcher had been right about one thing last night—

this whole mess was far from over. And she was still very much in the middle of it. It seemed he still didn't trust her, although he hadn't come right out and said it directly.

After a long five minutes of tenuous silence, Fletcher finally spoke. "How are your waffles?" he asked.

Suki began to lose patience. "You don't care how I feel about waffles," she announced, "so stop trying to make pleasant conversation to throw me off-balance."

He looked amused. "Is that what you think I'm trying to do?"

"That's exactly what you're doing. I've watched enough Perry Mason to know that old trick," she said adamantly. "You must think I'm an idiot or something."

That stopped him cold. "No, I don't think that." His eyes softened, and for a moment she was heartened, thinking he might return to his more winsome self. "I told you before, I'm not sure what to think. All I know is that there might be two million dollars hidden somewhere in this hotel."

"And you still believe I may have something to do with it?"

It took a second for him to answer. A second was a second too long, Suki thought. Then he shook his head slowly, but the gesture was decidedly unconvincing.

Suki almost got up and left, but she managed to keep her cool. "Is that why you were so eager to see me this morning? So you could interrogate me?"

Fletcher didn't answer, but he didn't back down.

He stared at her stonily, as if waiting for her to blurt out something that she might regret.

She drew herself up with dignity. "And I was hoping we had got past all that. I thought you were ready to trust me after last night."

"So did I," Fletcher said, drumming his fingers on the table thoughtfully. "Until Mr. Luchek gave me food for thought." He looked at her questioningly, but she had nothing to say. She had absolutely no idea what he was getting at. "Apparently," he continued reluctantly, "Mr. Luchek seems well acquainted with you. In fact, he intimated strongly that the two of you set up this whole thing together from the beginning."

Suki was so enraged that her hands shook, almost upsetting her glass. "How dare he!" she cried, her eyes throwing sparks. "And you believed him!" she said accusingly, turning her wrath on Fletcher. "You took the word of a common criminal over mine? And after he tied me up and threatened me!"

"Well, he claims that he tied you up because you were planning to run off with the loot and double-cross him."

"Well, it's not true!" She stood up, too angry to stay with him any longer. "Some detective you are," she said scathingly. "You believe everything you hear. Before we know it, *you'll* be in partnership with Luchek."

Fletcher watched this performance with evident interest. When she was finished, he put a hand on her arm and spoke with quiet authority. "Sit down, Suki."

"Let go of me," she commanded.

"Sit down," he repeated gently. "I didn't say I

believed him, did I?" His eyes caught hers and she saw a glimmer, just a glimmer, of the rapport that had linked them last night. Against her better judgment, she sat.

"That's better," he said. "Now, I take it you deny all this?"

"I certainly do."

"Good. Then I think it would be very beneficial to both of us if I hung around you for the next few days."

"Why?" she asked crossly. "Because you think I'm involved in a robbery?"

He sighed impatiently. "Look, Suki. The facts are quite obvious. You had the same suitcase as Luchek, the same flight as Luchek—"

"Circumstantial evidence," she said dismissingly.

"Is that another phrase you learned from Perry Mason?"

"Well, it's true, whatever it's called, and as far as I'm concerned, this has all been a gigantic and very unfortunate coincidence." Suki snapped her fingers and the waiter appeared, hovering over them. "Check, please."

The waiter put the bill next to Fletcher's plate, but before Fletcher could pick it up, Suki snatched it from under his fingers. "My treat," she said sardonically. Opening her purse, she reached for her wallet.

When she looked down, her gaze fell on the stack of money she had placed in her purse last night. The instantaneous recollection of how it had got there coupled with the shock of recognition caused her to snap her purse shut with undue haste.

But she wasn't fast enough. She looked up, startled and looking very guilty, as Fletcher's hand deftly intercepted her.

"What's the problem?" he asked, instantly alerted. Suki was trapped. The man had the instincts of a hawk. He quickly claimed her purse, opened it without looking at her, and found the money. He waved it in the air, fanning himself with it.

"I can explain that," Suki said weakly, but she knew as she said it that it was futile.

"Please do."

"I put it there last night—I mean when you came by—I didn't want you to know about the money, because I wasn't sure I could trust you." She struggled to articulate, but it was impossible.

Fletcher slowly flipped the money one bill at a time as he counted to himself. He looked up as if formulating his own conclusions. "Well, well," he said. "Ten thousand dollars. Did Luchek pay you off as well, or were you instructed to try your hand at bribing me after he failed?"

"Neither!" Suki cried.

"Oh, I see. You always like to carry this much cash around. Personally, I never leave home without my American Express card."

"Very funny," Suki said. "For your information, I put that money in there last night after I found the two million."

"Just sampling the goods, I suppose?"

"I already explained that. I was hiding it from you." Her face fell as she realized how ridiculous and false that must sound.

Fletcher didn't say a word.

"You don't believe me, do you?" she asked quietly.

"Would you?"

Suki thought that one over, and after a few seconds began shaking her head. If yesterday had started off badly, she thought, today had gone from bad to worse. What else could possibly go wrong now?

From that moment on, Fletcher never left Suki alone for more than a minute. Every time she turned her head, there he was watching her. He was maddeningly open about it, not even bothering to hide behind a newspaper or sneak along just out of sight nearby.

After breakfast, she doggedly decided to go for a solitary walk in the cool morning, hoping to be alone, and the plan succeeded—for a while. The tree branches overhead had a fat, thick covering of snow, and the snow on the trail was fresh, untouched by human footprints. Suki enjoyed the solitude as she strolled along, until suddenly she noticed another set of prints emerging from the woods. Her eyes followed them up the trail, and there was Fletcher, coyly waving hello.

She turned with a huff and headed all the way back to the lodge. After purchasing a book at the gift shop, she settled into a soft leather chair by the huge open fireplace in the middle of the room and tried to become engrossed in it; but the effort was futile. A hundred feet away, sitting in another chair, was Fletcher, passively reading. What made it all the more annoying was that he was reading the very same book she was! He caught her eye and held up his copy in a friendly manner to show it to her. Suki was not amused.

In a burst of defiance, she sprang up and ran to

the lobby and through the maze of hallways, determined to lose him. She quickened her pace, purposely taking the long way back to the exhibition hall where her sculptures were being displayed. This time, she noted with satisfaction, she was alone. For some reason, Fletcher hadn't followed, and for a good twenty minutes she worked alone, finishing to set up the final placards in front of each sculpture. Only the cop remained, waiting to be placed in front of the entranceway as her traditional opening piece. She had no sooner finished phoning a bellhop to come help her move it, when there was Fletcher, his arms wrapped around the statue's waist, hauling it to the front of the hall.

He adjusted the sculpture appropriately and gave her a self-assured smile, letting her know that this was only the beginning.

But Suki wasn't ready to give up. She left the exhibition hall quickly, this time ducking down a side stairwell used by the staff. She made her way through the underground maze of basement hallways and dark doorways, finally coming back up at the far end of the hotel. Fletcher was nowhere in sight. Flushed with triumph, she nevertheless took the added precaution of walking up three flights before taking the elevator back to her floor.

But when the elevator doors opened on thirteen, there stood Fletcher, arms folded, a mocking grin on his tanned face.

Without a word, Suki marched over to her room and closed the door behind her. When she emerged fifteen minutes later, she was dressed in a red-and-white skiing outfit. Fletcher was waiting for her, but he was still in his impeccable suit.

Together, they waited by the elevator in grandiose silence. When the doors opened, Suki marched in with Fletcher right behind. She looked at him, frowned in impatience, and stepped back into the hallway. Fletcher did the same. At her wit's end, Suki barely knew what to do. She couldn't keep stepping in and out of elevators all day long.

Suddenly, her face froze in fear. "Look," she said in a harsh whisper, pointing down the hall. "It's Luchek."

Fletcher jumped immediately in front of her, his body poised aggressively, but there was no Luchek.

It was a golden opportunity for Suki, and she quickly dashed into the open elevator just as the doors began to close. Fletcher turned, dumb struck, as she rode alone down to the lobby. She was sure he could hear her laughter echoing all the way back up the elevator shaft.

The ski rental was not crowded late in the morning, and Suki was fitted for a day on the slopes in a matter of minutes.

She cautiously peeked out the door before venturing outside. Hundreds of skiers were eagerly heading to the different ski lifts that dotted the mountain. Fletcher Colman was nowhere in sight. Happily, she put her feet in the bindings and snapped her skis on. Adjusting her sunglasses, she donned her gloves, put her hands through the ski-pole straps, planted herself firmly in position, and shoved off toward the lift. She desperately needed some time to herself, without having to worry about anything.

Joining the advanced-ski-lift line, she made her way along until it was her turn to get into position for a lift seat. She turned around to see the seat coming toward her and took one last apprehensive look around, feeling that Fletcher could still be somewhere nearby, watching her. She bent her knees in preparation, a sigh of relief coming over her as she dropped into the seat.

"This is a double ski lift," Fletcher's voice proclaimed as he practically materialized out of thin air. He dropped onto the seat just in time before it lifted choppily, trapping both of them in midair.

Suki almost fell off the lift from surprise, but Fletcher's quick hands prevented that. "Careful, there," he admonished. "It's a long way down." He pointed to the slopes below. His arms firmly around her, he brought the safety bar down in front of them.

Suki placed her skis on the foot holding and looked down to make sure they were steady. Instantly, her spirits lifted. Fletcher wasn't wearing skis at all. He was still dressed in a suit and a pair of expensive leather shoes.

"Nice ski outfit," she told him triumphantly. "I heard there's a wind-chill factor of ten below at the top of the mountain." She pointed to his shoes. "Are those the latest in skis?"

Fletcher didn't answer, but she knew he was in for it. The farther up the mountain they went, the colder it was going to get. In no time at all, they were greeted by a turbulent wind that caused Suki to zip her jacket up to her neck, and to readjust her wool hat over her ears. She turned to see how Fletcher was holding up.

Although he was putting on a good front, she could see that his hands were starting to turn red, and his ears were not far behind.

"Beautiful view," he said, pointing back down the

mountain. "I always like the peace and stillness at the summit of a mountain."

"Do you also like how cold it gets?" she couldn't help asking, more out of curiosity than a desire to needle him.

"It's good for the circulation," he said staunchly as he turned the flaps of his lapel inward. "Of course, now that you mention it, it is getting a bit cold. You wouldn't happen to have an extra pair of gloves on you or perhaps a scarf, would you? Or possibly a thick fur overcoat?"

Suki couldn't help laughing. "You're crazy, do you know that?" She was beginning to feel sorry for him, despite his earlier treatment of her, damn his crystal-blue eyes. "You could get pneumonia up here," she added.

"We'll be at the top soon enough," he said. "I'll be all right as long as I keep moving."

"You mean you'll be frozen stiff as a board." She removed her scarf and wrapped his hands in it. "Does that feel better?"

"Ahhh," he sighed. "Much better. I think I can feel the circulation returning." He took his right hand out and rubbed it on her rosy cheek. "But this is warmer," he said slyly.

She jerked his hand away, and it disappeared inside the scarf. Never in a million years was she going to let him see how much the simple, longing gesture had affected her. His touch was like lightning, even at subzero degrees in midair.

"The things I do for this job." He groaned and shook his head. "Sometimes it just isn't worth it." He mustered a smile and caught her eye. "Then again, here we are, just the two of us, trapped together. They say that two people can create a lot of body heat." He leaned closer to her, but she didn't move. She couldn't; there was no room to retreat on the skimpy seat.

"Good Lord," she said with a sudden revelation, "you were going to try and kiss me, weren't you?"

"Well, uh, yes," he admitted. "Now that you mention it, I was thinking along those lines. I thought it might take my mind off the fact that I'm being refrigerated, not to mention that you have a friendly face and seem to be mildly interested." He unwrapped the scarf from his hands and tied it around his neck so that it kept the lapels of his suit folded against his chest. "You'll have to forgive me," he said. "I certainly didn't mean to take liberties with you, but it's freezing up here."

Suki decided to forgive him. "That's quite all right," she said. "Just don't do it again."

"Hey, you two! Gate up!" the attendant shouted. They had reached the top of the lift.

They both whipped around in time to see the ramp only a few feet away. Suki pulled her skis off the lift and got the bar up, planting her feet on the ground in time to ski off safely. She expected Fletcher to ride the lift back down, but he jumped off doggedly, standing next to her in the snow.

She had no idea what he planned to do next. In a moment, she would be racing downhill on skis, and he would be abandoned on top of a mountain with nothing to do. She put on her sunglasses and peeked at him. He looked rather worried, she thought, as well he might. The sight of the steep slope was enough to make all but the most adept skiers nervous. And Fletcher wasn't a skier at all.

Suki grinned. "Race you to the bottom," she said wryly.

"What do I get if I win?" he called back to her.

She had to laugh.

"What do I get if I beat you to the bottom?" he repeated.

"Name it," she said expansively. "Anything you want. It's all yours."

"Would you spend the entire day with me, so that I don't have to keep following you?"

"Sure, why not?" She continued chuckling at his hopeless ploy. "But if I win," she added firmly, "you have to stop following me. Is that a deal?"

Fletcher unwound her scarf and strolled over to her, wrapping it around her neck and securing it in a tidy knot. "I assure you, I'll be at the bottom of this little hill before you're even halfway down."

Suki shook her head and laughed indulgently as she peered all the way down to where the ski lodge looked like a tiny matchbox and the skiers like little ants. "What are you going to do," she asked, "run all the way down the mountain?"

Fletcher looked at her solemnly. "I'll be waiting for you next to the skating rink," he said. "Look for a sign that says FINISH, and I'll be under it. Got that?"

Suki glanced over to the ski lift. "It's a ten-minute ride down," she reminded him. "You'd better get moving." And with that, she pushed off, confident that Fletcher would freeze to death before he was halfway there.

"Under the FINISH sign," he shouted down after her. "I'll be waiting for you."

She turned and looked back up, but he had vanished. Where does that man disappear to? she wondered. She glanced at the ski lift, thinking she would catch him riding down, but ten seats went by and he wasn't on any of them.

He had something up his sleeve, Suki mused as she readjusted her goggles. But it wouldn't do him any good. She headed back down, gathering momentum and relishing the thought of victory.

This time Fletcher was all bravado, she assured herself. He'd need a rocket to beat her. Then it dawned on her.

"Oh, Lord," she said aloud. "He'll use a bobsled!" The bet they had just made took on a sudden new meaning. Fletcher, damn his athletic record, had almost outsmarted her again. But this time she had a fighting chance, and she didn't intend to lose it. There was no time to waste, and she headed straight downhill, bending into the wind.

- 5 -

THE SMOOTH, ICY TOBOGGAN run glistened dangerously next to the slope, like a long, blinding mirror. Suki glanced at it nervously as the wind swept behind her sunglasses, making her eyes tear, but there was no way she wasn't going to at least try to beat him down the mountain. She was an excellent skier, but she was a little out of shape from too much work in the studio and not enough time on the slopes. Furthermore, Fletcher had awakened some competitive demon in her, one that wanted to wipe that confident smirk off his face. She didn't know what it was about him that made her want to show him up, unless it was simply that she wanted to impress him. But she had no reason to try to impress Fletcher Colman, she told herself firmly as she flew gracefully downward. No reason at all.

The course was more challenging than she had

bargained for, and she ordered herself to stay alert. Circumnavigating three moguls in a row, she barely managed to stay on her skis as a large, unseen bump threw her off-balance. The top part of the slope held only a few excellent skiers, all capable of steering clear of each other on the steep path. But the bottom part of the trail opened wider, where mixing the advanced skiers with beginners could cause trouble. Within minutes, Suki had cleared the top part of the course, but not without paying a heavy price for not warming up.

The merciless bumping had given her a headache, and her eyes were so watery that she was having trouble seeing the slope. She slackened her pace and allowed herself the luxury of gliding along a smooth, wide-open slope. Shearing across the mountain, she commanded a view of the entire ski area. To her left were expert skiers emerging from the same trail she had come from. To her right were the beginner's slopes, and next to that was the toboggan run.

Suki's eyes kept returning to the toboggan run, following its path as it weaved up and down and around the mountain. She watched in awe as a sleek sled tore like a rocket through a turn, straightening uneasily as it sped down the mountain at a furious pace that made her shiver.

"Definitely not a sport for the lighthearted," she muttered as she watched the sled whiz out of sight. "If Fletcher is going to race one of those, he must have nerves of steel."

Shaking her head, Suki turned out of her glide and aimed her skis straight down the mountain. If Fletcher had already finished his run he could be watching her this very minute, and she wanted him to see a good performance.

Her knees bent, she picked up speed and waited until the last minute before turning sharply away from a downed skier. By now, the bottom half of the slope was pocketed with intermediate and beginning skiers, making it appear like an obstacle course.

Too fast, she thought wildly as she narrowly missed a school of skiers. The instructor gave her a harried look, but she had no time to apologize. Down below, directly in her path, were two downed skiers, and she was forced to jam into a complete stop or risk running them over.

I'm losing valuable time, she worried.

Her thoughts were interrupted by the sound of a bobsled slamming around the final turn of the run on its way to the finish line. The rush of energy was awesome, commanding everyone on the slope to turn and follow its source. Fletcher, Suki thought resignedly. It must be him. Who else would hurtle down the track with such death-defying speed?

Coming out of the final turn, the sled was like a rocket out of a slingshot as it headed toward the finish-line banner that dangled between two poles. As the brakes were applied and a backlash of snow flew into the air, Suki watched nervously as a driver emerged.

But there wasn't just one passenger. There were four, all dressed alike in yellow-striped speed suits that made them resemble a family of bees. None of them could be Fletcher Colman, she noted with relief. They clambered out of the sled and pushed it off the course, slapping each other on the back as if to congratulate each other on a fine run.

Or on living to tell about it, Suki thought to herself. She glanced around the area, wondering if perhaps Fletcher was standing nearby or under a tree. But he was nowhere to be seen.

Heartened, Suki slapped her ski poles into the ground in a final effort to make sure she arrived at the finish line first.

Down a steep incline, past three slow skiers, around a mogul, over a mogul, through a group of slowpokes, Suki weaved faster and faster down the slope. A group of trees hid her view of the final approach, and she could only estimate that she was close to the end. She could no longer see the finish line banner or the toboggan course, but as she rounded the bottom of the hill she could see the bees pushing their sled.

Fletcher was not there.

"I beat him," she told herself exultantly, raising her poles in triumph, and let out a whoop that made the bees look up from their task of pushing their sled off the course.

She waved to the bees. "Just point me in the direction of the finish line, guys, and then get out of my way."

They looked at each other and then doggedly back at her as they continued to maneuver the heavy sled over the snowy hill.

Sure of her triumph, she didn't want to break her stride at the end. She tore into the last hundred yards with victorious pleasure. A small mogul stood between her and the bottom of the hill, and she aimed for it with the full intention of jumping off it for a rousing finale. She could still see the bees off to the side. They were continuing to push their sled, but suddenly they stopped to watch her with what looked like alarm. All at once they began yelling and waving their hands at her.

Suki thought they were toying with her. "Can't stop now, fellas," she called out, and bent her knees for the final jump. "Here I go!"

She never made it. A second later, one of the bees leaped out in front of her and tackled her around the waist.

"Ooof!" She felt the wind knocked out of her as she fell headlong into the snow, a tangle of arms and legs.

They both landed right next to the toboggan track, Suki on her back with the bee on top of her.

"You idiot!" she yelled at him. "You have a hell of a nerve—" Her voice was drowned out as a thunderous roar whizzed by her ear. She whipped her eyes to the side in time to see a new bobsled speed by, passing under the finish line only a few feet away.

Her face drained of color as she realized what had nearly happened to her.

"Oh, my God," she whispered. "I almost jumped right onto the course." She was still on her back, her rescuer looking down at her through the dark glass of his visor. The other men were shouting at her in Italian.

"I'm sorry," Suki said, trying to regain her composure. "I didn't realize—"

The men continued to shout in Italian, and Suki managed to pick up bits and pieces of what they were saying. It didn't take a genius to understand what they were telling her.

"There should be a warning sign around here," she said feebly. "This place is dangerous."

The man on top of her finally let her go, standing up and guiding her to her feet. He held her firmly around the waist, which was fortunate, since she was still so shaken from her near-accident that she felt like a rag doll. Efficiently, he began to brush the snow from her body in long, brisk strokes. Somehow it was comforting to be ministered to like this. She still didn't quite have her wits about her.

The man took off a glove and picked up her sunglasses, which were dangling from the side of her face. He put them back on properly, carefully wiping the snow from her hair.

"Thank you," she said with deep sincerity. "You saved my life." There was really nothing else she could say, and yet the few words seemed hopelessly inadequate.

The other men were still arguing, this time pointing to a huge, snow-covered board standing nearby. One of them gave it a swift kick, clearing it with a soft torrent of snow that fell to the ground. As he did, the hidden words of warning were uncovered: DANGER! NO SKIING—TOBOGGAN RUN

"Ahhh, bravo, bravo," they cheered.

Suki cast another grateful glance at the man standing next to her. "How do I say thank you in Italian?" she asked softly.

He turned from her, took off his helmet, and called to his comrades. "Hey, guys! How do you say thanks in Italian?"

Suki almost collapsed all over again. "Fletcher!" she shouted, staggered by her own surprise. "It was you!"

He turned around, helmet in hand, and with a glint in his eye gave her a hearty salute. "I'm glad I caught you when I did," he said calmly. "If I hadn't been there, it would have ruined our whole afternoon together—not to mention a nice chunk of your life."

Suki clapped a hand to her forehead. "You win," she conceded. "I never should have tried to outwit you." She stared at his outfit incredulously. "And where did you get that getup?"

Fletcher stood over her, his hands finding her shoulders and holding her gently. "These bees are very friendly. I think they took pity on me. And I wasn't trying to win anything, Suki. I'm only trying to establish a rapport between us. I wish you'd try to understand that." His eyes held hers with that sensual certainty that she knew she couldn't resist. But she had to *try* to resist it all the same. There was definitely something cagey about this man—maybe even dangerous. He was uncanny.

"You've got a very funny way of establishing a rapport," she said, mustering a self-righteous tone. "Have you ever considered how easy it would have been if you had simply trusted me in the first place?"

He actually stopped to think that over. "Trust, right?"

"It has been known to work wonders."

Suddenly, he bent his head and gathered her into his arms, pressing his lips to hers. He felt strong and warm and wonderful, but Suki reminded herself that this was definitely not the time or place. Besides, she had resolved to keep him at arm's length. "What—what are you doing?" she asked lamely, breaking away.

"Whatever happened to simple trust?" he asked with mock innocence.

She let out a long, slow breath. "It has to be developed slowly, over a period of time, like fine wine."

"I see."

But that kiss had got to her, and she was sure he knew it. Feeling less and less sure of herself, she turned and waved good-bye to the Italians. Then she slowly skied off, knowing that Fletcher couldn't follow.

"Hey!" he called out. "What about our afternoon together?"

She stopped and turned, considering. "It's still on," she answered. "Go rent yourself a pair of skis and meet me by the towrope after lunch."

"But I don't know how to ski!"

"I know!" Suki answered with a hearty laugh.

He looked so disappointed that she had to smother a giggle. "Couldn't we ice-skate instead?" he suggested.

"By the towrope, after lunch," she repeated, and with that headed off in the direction of the chair lifts, thinking she had managed to salvage some of her dignity. But when she stole a glance back at Fletcher, she saw that he was gamely heading over in the direction of the ski rental. The man was incorrigible. And she was going to have to face him, whether she wanted to or not.

The afternoon temperature had reached a warm thirty degrees when Fletcher finally showed up at the slope, looking indomitable with skis and poles held over his shoulder. He was dressed in navy ski pants and a navy sweater decorated with reindeer, which had obviously just been purchased. In addition to the new outfit, he sported a new pair of goggles, gloves, and an ear band. He looked exactly like an ad for sophisticated skiwear—except that he was a skier who would soon, she was sure, fall on his designer-clad bottom.

"How do I look?" he asked brightly.

Suki cut him a glance. "You look a lot better now than you will," she warned. "Beginning skiers take a lot of falls, you know."

"Not me," he assured her. "I've always been very adept at sports."

A few minutes later, after she had helped him into his ski bindings, Fletcher showed just how adept he was by skiing backward into a snowdrift.

"How do you stop?" he called to her just before taking his first plunge of the day.

Suki watched knowingly as he dropped right into the snowy pile, his skis flailing helplessly in the air.

"I think I'm going to enjoy this," she said to him as she watched him try to get back up. Each attempt he made only ended in his falling back into the drift.

Finally, snow dusted all over his face and clothes, he gazed at her imploringly and held out an outstretched hand. "Come on, give a guy a boost, will you?"

"Happy to oblige you." She skied over and stretched out a hand, but she quickly discovered that he had an ulterior motive. A second later, she had plunked down next to him in the drift, one leg flung over his, and her face and arms covered with light powder.

"You may be more experienced, but I'm still stronger than you are," he said gleefully.

She frowned loftily. "Now don't tell me you're going to resort to brute strength."

"Why not? It's all I've got at this point." His face was only inches from hers, and the temptation to stay close to him was strong. But now that she had the upper hand for a change, nothing was going to stop her from reveling in it. A feminine surge of power, one that she had never known she possessed, suddenly overcame her, and she immediately began to make delicious use of it.

"Great," she said sweetly, swinging her leg off his. "Let's see you do this." Using the angle of the slope for leverage, she sprang up neatly, leaning on her poles.

Fletcher watched her movements carefully and imitated them as best he could. He beamed as he righted himself, ready for the next instruction. "What's next?"

She favored him with a tiny smile and proceeded to instruct him. "Skiing," she said. "This time we'll go forward."

She gave him a few instructions on snowplowing and turning, which he absorbed with several avid nods. "It's just a simple towrope," she explained as they stood next to the moving rope. A little girl no more than five years old was waiting behind them impatiently. She had a riot of red curly hair, and was dressed in a white ski suit.

Fletcher looked down at her and smiled. "Would you like to get ahead of us, little girl?"

The child thought it over and shook her head.

"I think she wants to watch you do it first," Suki said. "Is that right, honey?"

The little girl nodded with a big, trusting smile at Fletcher.

"We're all waiting," Suki said.

Fletcher looked back and forth from one female to the other. "Terrific," he muttered. "I've just been elected the entertainment for the day." He looked once more at the child, who was watching him with large, round eyes. "Okay, I'm game. How do I manage this?"

"Gently hold the rope with one hand in front and the other in back, and hang on tight until you begin to move."

"Sounds easy enough, huh?" He shrugged, contemplated the moving rope, and took hold of it in his right hand. He examined his skis, making sure they were pointed up the small incline. "Tallyho," he said, and, squeezing the rope, was bolted forward right on his back. "Hey, stop this thing!" he yelled, looking back at Suki. His body was wiping the snowy ground as he continued to hold on to the rope.

Suki almost collapsed in laughter. "Try letting go!"

"I never thought of that," he yelled. He released the rope and rolled over into a sitting position, his body completely covered in powder. Looking up at her, he blew snow out of his face. "I suppose you purposely left out that simple instruction just to humiliate me."

"On the contrary." She pointed to the other beginners, who were managing perfectly well. "Most people know to let go."

"Yes, well, that's very nice for them, but I'm not most people." Using the technique she had just showed him, he leaned on his poles and boosted himself back up.

Suki gestured grandly to the towrope. "Care to try again?"

"But of course," he said, and carefully plowed back to the rope. The little redheaded girl was grinning at him again, and he gave her a dry look of his own. "Okay, let's see you try it," he said.

The little girl smiled obligingly, grabbed the rope, and easily headed up the slope, waving as she passed him by.

"A child," he intoned, looking at Suki and shaking his head. "She's probably been doing this all her life," he added defensively. "All five years."

The child arrived at the top, but instead of skiing back down, she beckoned for Fletcher to join her.

"That's just great," he said. "Now I've got a child prodigy giving me lessons."

"She likes you," Suki said. "Now come on, try it again."

He shook his head. "I think I need help."

She shook her head reluctantly and lined up behind him. "You can hold on to me."

"Exactly what I had in mind." He grinned, grabbing onto the rope with one hand and deftly slipping the other arm around her waist.

"If you can handle this rope with one hand all of a sudden, you don't need help," she said as they arrived at the top.

Fletcher grinned and said nothing. He adjusted his goggles and peered in calculation down the incline. "Ready when you are," he said jauntily.

Suki instructed. "Now, all you have to do is push off gently and snowplow down, leaning on first one foot and then the other."

He hesitated and looked at the red-haired girl. "Care to demonstrate?"

"Sure, mister." With a toothy grin, the child easily skied down the incline until she reached the bottom, where she turned and waved at him gaily.

The little girl bowed extravagantly, obviously expecting lavish praise, and Suki and Fletcher both applauded enthusiastically as she bowed again. "Brava!" he called to her. She flung out an arm in invitation, telling him to join her.

"Well, here goes nothing," he muttered.

Suki nudged him on. "Ready, set, go!" He took off, and she skied alongside him, expecting him to fall awkwardly at any moment, but Fletcher moved gracefully after her, mastering the simple slope with ease and coming to a perfect stop. The little girl greeted him as if she hadn't seen him in twenty years, hurrying over to him and throwing her arms around his knees.

"Very good!" she said importantly. "You get a gold star!"

Fletcher seemed to agree with her. "That was great," he announced, lifting the child into his arms and beaming at her approvingly. "Let's do it again."

Suki laughed. "That was good," she admitted. "I think you're getting the hang of this."

"I'm an expert ice skater," he said with animation, putting the little girl back down. "The technique is the same, isn't it?"

"I wouldn't know," Suki admitted honestly. "I've never skated."

"Never?" Fletcher asked, suddenly very interested. His face lit up with the seeds of revenge.

An hour later, having finished skiing, Suki found herself trying to keep her fingers warm while lacing up her rented ice skates. "Stupid, stupid, stupid," she admonished herself. "Why couldn't I keep my big mouth shut?"

"Stop complaining," Fletcher said. "Besides, I'll be next to you the whole time. You'll love it."

She finished lacing, and looked up at him. If he had been tentative before, he was now the epitome of strength and grace in black figure skates. Behind him was the huge skating rink, surrounded by mighty mountains. It was a daunting sight.

Fletcher guided her onto the ice and held her firmly around the waist. His control seemed effortless, and she hung on to him for dear life. They walked around the rink three times until she got the hang of it.

"It's easy," Suki said with more confidence than she felt, but she spoke too soon. Losing her balance, she slid helplessly, grabbing at the air for support. Fletcher caught her neatly, locking her tightly against his lean, hard body. Suki was keenly aware of his superior strength and agility, and although she wouldn't have admitted it for the world, at this moment she was very glad of them.

"I'd better hold on to you for a while longer," he said, as if the idea appealed to him more than was necessary. Together, they made their way around, gliding in unison until they developed a slow, gentle rhythm.

The gentle, persistent wind blew around them, putting roses into her cheeks, and her long black hair waved behind her as they gradually picked up speed. Neither of them said anything for a while, letting their movements flow together to create a new harmony between them. It was a harmony that would have been there from the beginning, Suki suspected, if it hadn't been for the outlandish circumstances in which they had met. This is how it should have been, she thought dreamily. They made a sharp turn, and a lock of hair fell across her face. Fletcher reached over and gently brushed it aside, letting his fingers caress her rosy cheek.

"Lovely hair," he said in a low voice.

Her heart jumped. "Thank you."

"It's the first thing I noticed about you yesterday when you walked into the hotel lobby."

Suki was surprised. "You saw me when I checked in?"

Fletcher nodded. "I make a habit of noticing unusual people."

"Oh." Well, this was an interesting piece of news. She proceeded carefully, sure that she was going to hear something she would like. "And you found me unusual?"

His eyes twinkled. "Not at all. It was that ridiculous suitcase of yours with that pyramid painted on the side."

She laughed and gave him a playful punch, by now accustomed to the fact that her outlandish luggage had caused such a tangle of misunderstandings. True, it had got her into trouble, but without it, she wouldn't have met Fletcher and she wouldn't have been caught up in his whirlwind life.

"It is an eye-catcher, all right," she admitted wryly. "That's exactly why I bought it. So that I wouldn't have to waste time in airports examining luggage to be sure which one was mine." She laughed again. "I guess the plan backfired, though."

"Not necessarily." He said no more, and she decided to leave it at that. The last thing she wanted was to dwell on the case again, and she could sense that he was as reluctant as she was. Her spirits lifted immeasurably. He did like her, no matter what his suspicions. And in time everything would straighten out. She had to believe that.

They made their way along the ice, Suki holding on to his arm with both hands. The afternoon was too pleasant to spoil. Then Suki noticed a sunny, familiar face.

"Don't turn around," she said merrily, warning Fletcher. "We're being followed."

Fletcher's face instantly became hard and alert. "I already knew," he said tautly, without looking. "I didn't want to alarm you."

Out of nowhere, the little redheaded girl passed by them, skating backward. "Hi!" she called. When she saw Fletcher she smiled broadly and did a complete figure-eight around them before taking off again.

Suki could feel Fletcher's tension dissolve. "Oh, so that's who you meant," he said. "I thought—" He stopped short as the little girl came back and skated alongside them, smiling up at Fletcher.

Suki spoke into his ear. "I think she has a crush on you."

His eyes glinted suddenly. "Well, she's not the only one."

She drew back from him slightly, risking a fall. "Oh, is that so?" she asked archly. "Well, don't be so sure."

"Listen to me, please." His tone was urgent. "I'm only thinking of your safety."

That made no sense, unless he was dwelling on

the case again, and her temper flared. "Is that all you can think about?" she demanded.

"Maybe so," he said. "But until I get to the bottom of this, you are not to get out of my sight."

Suki's mouth dropped open. "You're crazy, do you know that? Every time I think you're finally coming to your senses about me, you do an about-face and turn into an interrogator. How many times do I have to repeat, I'm not involved with that stolen money."

"Ah, but you are," he said sternly. "And whether it's simply by accident or choice, one thing is certain, you're in danger." He held her tightly as they made another turn.

"Look over my right shoulder," he commanded her. "At the skating house. Do you see a familiar face?"

Suki obeyed and glanced over to where skaters were coming in and out of the small skating lodge. "I don't see any—" Her face paled suddenly as she saw the sinister man sitting leisurely on a bench just off to the side. "It's Luchek!"

Luchek had a pair of binoculars around his neck, and as Suki watched, he lifted them up and looked right at her.

"He's spying on us right now!" She turned away immediately, and looked into Fletcher's eyes for an explanation.

"He was following you all morning," Fletcher explained. "And all afternoon we were never out of his sight."

Suki felt sick. "I was wondering why you weren't following *him*." She cast another uneasy glance back at Luchek. "Why is he following me?"

Fletcher's mouth tightened. "That's the first of two questions I need answered."

"What's the second question?"

He broke away from her suddenly, letting her skate on her own. The unexpected freedom was unnerving but exhilarating. She found that she could actually skate on her own. Gaining momentum, she sailed along the ice, her arms out for balance, when suddenly she realized that she didn't know how to stop. Fletcher stood still and watched her with a knowing smile, waiting to see what she would do.

Suki had only one choice. She aimed straight at Fletcher, heading toward him like an arrow. He stood still, waiting for her, and when she reached him she crashed right into him, letting him break her stride. She came to an abrupt halt, looking up at him breathlessly. "Thanks," she gasped.

"Anytime."

"But Fletcher . . . what was the second question?" She was still pressed up against him, his hands holding firmly on to her arms.

"Oh, that," he said with a shrug. "I was wondering what Luchek would do if he saw us do this." Without another word, he bent down and kissed her thoroughly, molding her body to his and claiming her mouth as if they were quite alone and had all the time in the world. Suki clung to him instinctively, surprised at how easily he could arouse her, even in the middle of a skating rink. She wished suddenly that they were truly alone, that they could go on kissing like this indefinitely. Fletcher let the kiss last for a good long minute before breaking it, looking down into her flushed face.

"What was that for?" she gasped. "What are you doing?"

"Well," he said mischievously, "as long as we're being watched, I thought we might as well give him a good show."

- 6 -

SUKI DRESSED EVEN MORE CAREFULLY for her showing that evening than she had for the day on the slopes. This was the last stop on her tour, and she wanted to be prepared in the event of a small miracle. One never knew when an important art critic might show up, or a collector with a lot of money and the right eye. She had just slipped into her evening dress, a vision in black tulle with no sleeves and no back, when Fletcher knocked briskly on her door. She opened it with a flourish, and was delighted to see him decked out gallantly in a tuxedo. He wore it with masterful grace, as if the classic male garment had been invented especially for him.

"Suki, you look radiant," he said, his eyes sweeping languidly over the clouds of tulle that did not quite conceal her curves.

"Thank you," she whispered, suddenly apprehensive, as if expecting to see Donald Luchek lounging only a few feet away.

"Oh, don't worry," Fletcher said cheerfully, reading her thoughts. "Our friend Luchek is holed up in his room. He hasn't left it since dinner. The bell captain promised to inform me the minute he does."

Suki breathed an audible sigh of relief. "You think of everything, don't you?"

He lifted an eyebrow. "At the moment, everything that I'm thinking has just been dimmed by the way you look in that dress." He reached out and touched her bare shoulders, molding them under his strong hands. Suki caught her breath. His hands moved to cup her chin as he examined her face intently. "You're still nervous," he observed, kissing her forehead and then her mouth. "Don't be. Everything is under control."

She shook her head, refusing to let thoughts of Luchek interfere with what promised to be a most exciting evening. Together, they walked to the door, Suki's hand resting lightly on Fletcher's arm. "It's not that," she insisted. "I'm thinking about my career. This is my last show on this tour, and so far nothing monumental has happened."

"Happened?" He frowned, not understanding. Then he figured it out. "Oh, you mean like selling a sculpture, or something like that?"

"Something like that," she repeated wryly. "This little publicity tour has reduced my savings account drastically."

The elevator doors opened, and Fletcher guided her inside. He seemed quite attentive suddenly, as if what she was saying was of utmost importance. "You are very talented," he said. "Eventually the whole world will know about you, and then, who knows, maybe fame and fortune will follow."

Suki laughed, pleased at his support, but wanting to face the truth. "Please, don't throw platitudes at me, Fletcher."

"No, no. I mean that sincerely."

She smiled. "You're just trying to cheer me up." They exchanged a warm glance. "Thanks, but—

"What I'm trying to do is have a simple conversation with you about art—yours, to be precise. I'm very interested in your work."

"Oh." She brightened, but then she frowned. "Well, there's a lot more to it than that, unfortunately." It was impossible to explain to him all at once. "Talent isn't the only thing that matters," she said. "There are also things like connections, perseverance, luck—"

"I'm just making a prediction," he said, undaunted. "Besides, I like what you do. And I think that if I like it, others will, too."

Suki grinned. "But you *know* me, Fletcher. You're not objective."

"No, I'm not," he said with a shrug. "So what? I like you, and I want you to do well. What's wrong with that?"

She beamed at his words, but she also wanted him to understand. "What's wrong is that it's not realistic. What I do, Fletcher, is try to eke out a living teaching part-time at the local university, while pursuing a dream."

"I know all that already," he said. "Remember, I had you checked out thoroughly." He touched her arm. "But why are you so down on yourself all of a sudden?"

Suki sighed again and looked at him wryly. "Are you always so good at getting people to come forth with the truth?"

"It's good for the soul," he said softly, watching her. "Only I don't think you know the whole truth."

"Oh, I know it all right. I knew it before I even started out on this foolhardy adventure. I'm just another young hopeful who thinks she deserves recognition. This whole eight weeks of touring has been nothing more than an egotistical attempt at self-promotion." She nodded firmly. "I know that."

"Well, I don't know," he said, taking her arm and looking down at her earnestly. "What you do is unique. You're an original, and your art reflects a literal realism."

Suki turned to him, amazed, as the elevator doors opened and they stepped out. "That's right," she said. "That's exactly what I'm trying to do." He smiled knowingly, and she laughed. "Where did you learn that lingo, anyway? Fletcher Colman, you continue to surprise me. I'm impressed."

"There's more," he announced smugly. "And it has a happy ending."

"There is?" She gave him a joyous little laugh. "Go on. You're batting a thousand."

He was delighted to oblige. "Well, let's see. In your work, you—uh, re-create familiar American types through a heightened reality."

She hung onto his glib words, spellbound. "Fletcher . . . I had no idea you were so interested—not to mention perceptive—about my work. I'm flattered. I really am."

"Well, I do have an eye," he said.

"Yes, but you described my work as though you were an expert."

He laughed suddenly. "All right, you caught me. I got most of that fancy speech out of the latest copy of *Art World.*"

"Oh, sure you did." Suki chuckled. "*Art World,* right?" She continued laughing, shaking her head, and Fletcher smiled back, shrugging at the whole thing as if it were a big joke.

"That is the name of the magazine, isn't it?"

"Oh, yes, that's the name, all right. But I doubt if you would ever read about me in that magazine."

Fletcher smiled triumphantly. "Well, you're wrong," he said. "That's exactly where I read it."

"Oh, I see," she said, playing along. "And I suppose *Art World* was so interested in little old me that they dedicated their entire cover story to my sculptures."

"Not quite. But maybe one day they will."

She grabbed his arm, reached up, and kissed him on the cheek.

"What was that for?" he asked, looking startled but very pleased.

"For having faith in me. For saying what you said. I appreciate the vote of confidence. At this point in my life, it's exactly what I need to keep my spirits up."

"Oh, really? Well, I'm very glad to hear that, because you can read it for yourself whenever you need an ego boost." To her utter amazement, he produced a clipping from *Art World*. She looked, and saw that it was an article with a picture of her policeman sculpture at the top. "It's the latest issue," Fletcher added.

Suki was frozen speechless, unable to think. Her eyes scanned the article, reading so quickly that the words scarcely made sense. Fletcher took it from her patiently and began to read it aloud.

"'Suki Lavette's ability to mold plastic to the texture of human skin and all its frailties was delightfully evident to this critic. In fact, I found myself standing nervously with arms raised, shouting at the policeman not to shoot.'" He put down the article and smiled. "Sounds familiar, doesn't it?"

Suki was clutching his arm for support. "I can't believe it. I just can't believe it. So *that's* who that photographer was in San Francisco." She trilled a nervous little laugh. "And I thought he was just some tourist."

"Apparently not. If connections are as important as you say, then you'll have to start learning some of these people by face, not just by name," he pointed out. "You don't want to miss someone important." She nodded breathlessly, still overcome by her write-up. "Now come on," he said. "The rising young artist doesn't want to be late."

The hurried along through the lobby, Suki feeling a new surge of excitement and energy. As they approached the gallery, she caught the cover of the latest *Art World* at a newsstand. Perusing it briefly, she saw that there was no mention of her name anywhere on the outside. This meant that Fletcher had bought a copy without knowing what was inside. They slowed down before the entrance to the showing, where the policeman stood watch. People were admiring it and making the usual comments, but Suki was only interested in one thing.

"Why did you buy that magazine, Fletcher?"

He smiled down at her. "I'm interested in you. You're interested in art. The magazine was there. So I bought it."

Suki couldn't believe the warm sense of gratification that spread through her like butter on a warm day. "You know something?" she said coyly. "I think you're really beginning to like me."

"Of course I like you, you adorable girl," he answered. "But I still have a job to do."

"Oh. So you're not just stringing me along to pry information out of me?" she blurted out, knowing it was the wrong thing to say and regretting it instantly.

He reacted with the dry, ironic stare she had already come to know so well, one eyebrow slightly raised and his fine, sensual mouth set into a tight little line. He studied her at leisure for a long, embarrassing moment as if deciding just what to do with someone as impossible as her. Then he stepped forward decisively and swept her into his arms, leaving no room for argument or protest. With complete mastery, he leaned over and took her mouth, kissing her with total abandon, as if he were a soldier about to head off to war.

They kissed for a long, shameless time, Suki's heart pounding madly. People were staring at them, but she didn't care.

"You seem to be making a habit of this," she gasped the moment she caught her breath.

"It's the only way to handle you when you say something impossible," he informed her. "Besides," he added with a mysterious air, "I was looking for clues."

"I see. And did you find any?"

"I always do," he said, eyes narrowed, and, still

holding her close, he kissed her once more for good measure. "Come on," he said, taking her by the hand. "It's time everyone met the latest darling of the art world."

They walked inside, and Suki muffled an exclamation at the size of the crowd. It was the largest one she had drawn by far, a mixture of skiers, people from the town, and others who seemed to be knowledgeable about what they were looking at. Suki smiled to herself. Leaving the policeman outside as an advertisement always did the trick. People would stop in alarm when they saw it, and then they would realize what it was and be drawn inside by curiosity.

The showing continued much like any other, with viewers filing in and out all evening. Suki waited for the curator of the Museum of Modern Art in New York to rush over and exclaim over her, proclaiming her the find of the century, but as usual, nothing out of the ordinary happened. Suki had planned the tour for maximum visibility. The idea was to make sure the notables in the art world would be able to view her works as conveniently as possible. In eight weeks, she had gone through New York City, Dallas, Atlanta, Chicago, and San Francisco. Vail was really just an excuse to finish off the tour with some fun and relaxation. The entire trip also included promotional letters inviting local critics to view her work. Some came, most didn't. And even when they did, the most she had received were small write-ups lost in the back pages of daily papers.

With her savings totally depleted and her hopes almost gone, the write-up in *Art World* was the first clue that her efforts had succeeded. Vail was the last chance actually to sell something, and she prayed that the prestigious write-up would bring a fresh, new face, one with clout and money to spend.

Suki circled the gallery all evening, listening to the usual array of comments.

"So real."

"Looks just like my Uncle Leo."

"Hey, George, take a picture of me under arrest. You got the cop in focus?"

"They're just like mannequins in a store window. What's so arty about that?"

Suki smiled politely at everything people said, even the less-than-flattering remarks. She and Fletcher exchanged an occasional aside as they circled the room and listened, and she found that she enjoyed the showing much more with a friend along. It was easy to imagine that they were a pair of secret agents casing the crowd, traveling under assumed identities. All they needed was a pair of walkie-talkies so that they could communicate from opposite sides of the room.

"Rich dentist interested in the boxer," he murmured to her in a clipped shorthand as they crossed paths near the door.

"Forget the dentist," she murmured back a few minutes later. "He's going to an auction in New York tomorrow."

Even with Fletcher along, she eventually resigned herself to the inevitability that nothing wonderful was going to happen, when she became aware of a pair of sharp, piercing eyes that glowed from the face of a very distinctive-looking young man. He was dressed in an old-fashioned starched white shirt with cuff links, oversized gray trousers, outlandish red-and-gray suspenders, and a red bow tie. Suki had noticed him come in earlier that evening, but unlike most people, who left after about twenty minutes of looking around, he had remained for a long time—too long, she thought nervously. Each time he finished a long perusal of one of her sculptures, she would catch him eyeing her with deep curiosity. Her uneasiness grew and grew, until after a while it seemed to her that there must be something sinister about him. Luchek, she thought wildly. He must be a front for Luchek. Panicking, she looked around for Fletcher, but he wasn't anywhere to be seen.

Then she saw him talking to two young couples, amused and curiously flattered to hear him giving them a sales pitch. "It's a wonderful investment," he was saying earnestly, indicating the article in *Art World*. "She's going to be one of the big names."

The couples were actually nodding, and Suki hesitated to interrupt. She waited until the two couples moved off, and then she grabbed Fletcher's arm.

"Hi," he said, looking down at her with lambent blue eyes. "How's it going?"

Suki leaned closer to him. "I'm—not sure," she said in a low voice. She stole a glance backward, and saw that the odd-looking young man was watching her again. "Look at me and don't turn around," she commanded. "He's there."

Instantly Fletcher was on guard, his eyes flashing. "Luchek?"

"No, not Luchek, his accomplice."

"Accomplice?" Fletcher tensed and tried to turn around, but Suki stopped him.

"Don't look," she said frantically. "He'll see you." She threw her eyes quickly off to the side. The man was gazing directly at them. When he saw her look at him, his eyes darted away, and he began retreating toward the door.

"There," Suki said quickly, pointing to the entrance. "Hurry, he's getting away! The man with the suspenders. You can't miss him."

Fletcher darted instantly to the door, his body moving with lithe energy. He disappeared for a second, and then Suki heard an indignant shout.

"Ow!" The voice was not Fletcher's. "Unhand me this instant, you—you—Neanderthal."

Fletcher emerged back in the doorway, the smaller man wedged under one arm. He was holding him in some sort of painful armlock that made the man wince. The crowd parted at once, apprehensive and curious.

"Is this the man?" Fletcher asked her maintaining his grip.

Suki nodded vigorously. "He's been watching me all night long with those beady little eyes."

"Let go of me!" the man demanded. "This instant."

Suddenly, Detective Spalding appeared out of nowhere. "I'll handle this."

Fletcher released the man and Spalding grabbed him by the collar. "What did he do, molest someone?"

The man eyed the hotel detective haughtily. "My dear fellow, the only molesting being done at the moment is your beefy hand on my lapel. Would you kindly remove it at once?"

Spalding gave him a dirty look. "Oh, a wise guy, huh?"

"Why were you following me?" Suki demanded.

The man gave Spalding another withering glance,

and Spalding released his hold. When at last he was free, he adjusted his collar and reached inside his lapel. Both Spalding and Fletcher flinched, and the man froze.

"That better be a cigarette you're reaching for," Spalding said.

"I don't smoke," he replied. He continued to fish inside his breast pocket, and at last he took out a business card and handed it to Suki.

When she read it, her face dropped. "Oh, no! Oh, my God. I'm terribly, terribly sorry," she said. "Can you ever forgive me?"

Spalding was now angry. "What do you mean sorry? I thought you said this man was a pervert or something."

"I only said he was following me."

"And so I was."

Fletcher's eyes flashed. "So, you admit it?"

The man shrugged. "So, I admit it. That is not just cause for a display of physical abuse, is it?"

Spalding drew himself up. "Is anyone going to prefer charges here?"

The man looked pleasantly at Suki and smiled. "The only thing I prefer is a glass of champagne."

"Coming right up," Suki said, relieved at the chance for something to do, and she made a beeline for the bar. Fletcher was right on her heels.

He caught up to her just as she was ordering three glasses. "Who the devil is he? What's going on?"

Suki faced him excitedly, her face radiant. "Zeebo Molinari," she explained. "He's a very well-respected art agent."

Fletcher's face showed immediate comprehension, and he put out his hand to stop the bartender from pouring the champagne. He examined the label of the bottle and changed the order. "Make that Moët," he said. "Or the best you've got."

Suki was speechless. Leave it to Fletcher to come through at a time like this.

"This is your big chance," he said, "don't cheapen it with a second-rate champagne."

She nodded. "You're right. I can't afford it, but it's worth it."

He gave her a fast, gentle kiss. "My treat."

Suki summoned her considerable poise and walked gracefully back to where Zeebo Molinari was still standing with Spalding, looking as if he would rather be somewhere else. She quickly handed him a glass, and Fletcher offered one to Spalding, who shook his head.

"I don't drink on duty," he said. "If you'll excuse me." He left quickly, and Suki could tell that he was relieved to be out of the whole situation.

"Moët would have been wasted on him anyway," Molinari observed. Suki gave Fletcher a grateful glance, which he returned with a smile. Molinari got right down to business. "You're without representation at this time?"

"Uh—that's right." Or at any time, she added silently.

"I find your work very exciting, Ms. Lavette."

"Oh, please, call me Suki. And this is Fletcher Colman," she added politely. "I'm sorry if he—"

"I hope you'll forgive me," Fletcher broke in smoothly. "There's been a little—uh, disturbance in this hotel, and we don't want a new artist with Suki's talent to run into any trouble, do we?"

Molinari looked at Fletcher with new respect. "I

see. Well, no harm done." He broke into a smile, which heartened Suki immensely. "You'll have to show me that armlock sometime, Mr. Colman. I may be able to use it when I'm besieged by young hopefuls." They exchanged a look of understanding. "Now, if you'll excuse me, I'd like to speak to Ms. Lavette about her work."

"Of course." Suki reflected that Fletcher could be utterly suave and persuasive when he wanted to be. He had practically attacked Zeebo Molinari, and now the two men were shaking hands before the reputed agent led her away.

"I'd like to talk to you about the possibility of an auction at Barnaby's," he said.

"Barnaby's!" Suki was thrilled. "Really? But, Mr. Molinari, do you really think I'm ready for that?"

"Call me Zeebo. And yes, I think you're more than ready. In fact, it's exactly what you need to get the attention you deserve."

Suki peeked over her shoulder at Fletcher. He toasted her with his glass, his eyes sparkling with excitement for her. As she and Zeebo discussed the details of his plan and the impossible began to take shape and turn into reality, she realized again how supportive and loyal Fletcher had been. He still wasn't sure who or what she was, and yet he had helped her in every way he could. Their eyes met and she gave him her warmest smile.

An hour later, Zeebo had gone, and there were only a few stragglers left in the gallery. "I did it!" Suki shouted, impulsively throwing her arms around Fletcher as they rode up to her room.

Fletcher laughed and ran his hands seductively down her back.

"An auction!" she said proudly. "I can hardly believe it."

"I told you," he said smugly, but he was smiling, obviously as pleased as she was at her success.

"And at Barnaby's, of all places." She said the name reverently, hardly daring to believe it was true.

Fletcher turned her around and gathered her close. "Congratulations." He looked down at her for a long while, and their eyes shone as a single unit. When he kissed her, it was with a certainty that almost took her breath away. She felt giddy and light-headed, bubbling with new effervescence.

The elevator doors opened, and she looked at him silently. Together, they walked down the hallway to her room, the sudden quiet only intensifying the anticipation that was jumping inside of her. Suki's hands fumbled as she tried to get the key into the lock. "I don't know how I'm every going to sleep tonight," she said breathlessly. "I'm too excited."

"Then perhaps it isn't time to sleep." He spoke huskily, turning the key in the lock for her and gently opening the door. Her heart was pounding.

She walked inside ahead of him, stopping in the middle of the room, suddenly shy now that they were alone. Fletcher came up quietly behind her, holding her gently as he nuzzled her hair. "You are beautiful," he murmured.

She took in a sudden sharp breath and closed her eyes, fired with the knowledge of his passion.

"I have a good idea." He released her and walked over to the phone, dialing room service. "A bottle of your best champagne, please." In response to Suki's surprise, he added, "We have something to celebrate."

"You do have style," Suki said as he hung up the phone.

"Thank you." His eyes raked over her body, sending a shaft of heat coursing through her. "I propose a bottle now, and another after the auction is over."

"The auction? You're coming to the auction?" Suki asked, startled.

"Of course. This is a major turning point for you. I wouldn't miss it for the world." His unquestioning encouragement warmed her like a midsummer sun, and she was flooded with the urge to melt into his arms.

"But I'm still an unknown," she said weakly, knowing that words were about to abandon her altogether. Her eyes were lit from within, twin fires burning in invitation.

"Not to me." He walked forward purposefully, his desire written plainly on his face.

Suki looked up at him, knowing that this was inevitable, and wanting it to happen as much as she had ever wanted anything. She didn't yet understand how or why this man had been destined to so affect her life, nor could she be sure that she would ever understand it. But it didn't matter. Nothing mattered except the line of electricity that ran from his eyes to hers, uniting them on a single current of expectation.

"Kiss me," she murmured boldly, and he complied, taking her mouth with lush, sensual abandon. They kissed for a long, delicious time, his hands luxuriating in her hair. The taste between them was sweet and dusky, reminding her dimly of languid summer nights.

He guided her gently to the bed without lifting his mouth from hers, sitting her down and still kissing her as his hands moved to her shoulders. The golden straps of her gown, flimsy as gossamer, fell willingly at his touch, sliding helplessly down her slender arms. At last he lifted his mouth from hers and looked at her gravely. The demanding passion in his eyes thrilled her.

Suki began to tremble from anticipation. She wanted him fiercely, wanted him to possess her long into the night, but she also knew that a long, slow approach would be much more fulfilling this first time than a wild, reckless one. So she sat facing him, her eyes luminous and bright, her finely cut mouth parted, waiting for him to make the next move.

Without taking his eyes from hers, he reached over and drew the straps all the way down, taking the top of the bodice with them to slowly reveal her breasts. His hands grazed her breasts as he did this, sending them into taut peaks of response. She gasped slightly, her eyes fluttering to a close, and he made a long, masculine sound of appreciation.

"Lovely," he said, gazing at her beauty. His hands reached out slowly and covered her breasts. He sighed. "And so impossibly soft."

Holding her back with one hand, he bent down to take one rosy peak into his mouth. The gentle, insistent teasing sent her into a whirlpool of pleasure, igniting her intensely. He moved from one breast to the other, not allowing her to fall back on the bed, enjoying the velvety firmness of her breasts as he aroused them.

Suddenly, the magic was shattered by the ringing of the phone. "Ignore it," she pleased.

"I can't," he whispered raggedly. "I left the

number here, just in case. It might be important." Suki bit back her surprise and disappointment. He had actually left her room number. Was he merely covering his bases, or was he being unforgivably presumptuous? It was impossible to tell with him; he was hot one minute and cold the next. She watched as he reached out blindly and groped for the receiver, finding it and barking a quick "yes?" into it. His face changed rapidly as he listened. "Thank you," he said tersely a moment later, and hung up in a hurry. "I've got to go."

Suki couldn't believe her ears. "Go? But why?"

"That was the bell captain. Luchek just checked out of the hotel."

"But . . . but . . ."

"No buts about it. I'm still on the job. The case comes first."

Suki lifted the front of the gown to cover her bare breasts, her face crumbling. She was so confused that she hardly knew what to think. He was protecting her safety, and yet he had no qualms about dashing off in the middle of making love to her. It didn't really make sense, and there was no time to discuss it. He was moving like a minuteman running off to fight the redcoats.

It wouldn't have been so bad, if only he would say something, reassure her, tell her when he would see her again. She was dying to ask him that, but pride held her back. She wanted him to offer that information himself. He had said he would see her at the auction, but . . .

Fletcher was already at the door. He whipped around and smiled briskly, already all business. It was amazing how quickly he had transformed himself, she thought, just like an actor changing roles. The mental comparison stung her, and she stared at him doubtfully as he opened the door. "Take care of yourself," he said, blowing her a kiss. Then he left without a backward glance.

- 7 -

BARNABY'S OF SAN FRANCISCO was the sort of place Suki had fantasized about, but she had never dreamed of actually having her own work auctioned there. It was a huge, ever-changing museum of collectibles, all displayed for one purpose and one purpose only. They were all destined for the auction block after a week on exhibit.

Her policeman sculpture had been shipped hurriedly, providing customers with only a last-minute viewing. But Zeebo assured her that there would be a large gathering as long as he had anything to do with it. He was true to his word; on the day of the auction the place was packed. The policeman stood in a prominent place, surrounded by works from other artists of various distinction.

"Excellent," Zeebo commented as he looked around the gallery. "I think we got the best spot."

Suki smiled eagerly as they walked over to one side, watching a large group inspect the policeman. "Should I say anything?" she asked. "I mean if they ask questions?"

"Of course." Zeebo patted her hand. "Be cordial, but above all else, be yourself. Just don't be nervous. After all, you have me here."

He stepped confidently into the crowd and took the opportunity to launch into his selling spiel. His bright yellow bow tie and tux contrasted with Suki's flowing purple and white gown trimmed with narrow gold braid, giving her the effect of a Grecian maiden.

The potential buyers sported all kinds of garments, from staid business suits to leather alligator pants and fantastic headdresses. It was definitely a mixed group, Suki thought as she surveyed the crowd. Art like hers attracted all kinds.

Zeebo handled questions deftly, initiating discussions and getting people excited about her work. Watching him in action, Suki was doubly grateful that he had approached her. He certainly knew what he was doing. There was only one thing missing.

Fletcher. She told herself a hundred times that it was foolish to expect him to show up, that he hadn't really meant it when he had said he would be at the auction; that, when it came down to it, they had only been two ships passing in the night. He'd probably caught up with Luchek by now, she reasoned, and had gone back home. Suki Lavette would be just ancient history to him.

"Have you ever displayed at Girelle's?" someone asked her. It was the man in the alligator pants. "I could have sworn I've seen this style before."

"Uh—no," she answered, trying not to stare at

his peculiar attire. He stood back for a moment, showing off his outfit, and she realized that he wanted people to stare. That was the whole point. She managed a weak smile and turned as another of Zeebo's friends pounced on her. It was a woman in a chic white dress with a severe hairdo.

"Haven't I seen you in SoHo?" she asked, preparing to jot the answer down on a small pad.

Suki regarded this woman with respect, as she was obviously a serious collector. "Yes," she answered cordially. "I had a show there at the beginning of my tour."

"An interesting subject," someone else was saying. "I'd love to display that cop near my new Warhol."

"Yes," the woman with the pad added. "It would do well alongside my Brancusi in the study."

"Or in the front yard," a new voice added wryly, "where it could not only grace the lawn, but deter nocturnal burglars as well."

Suki lit up. "Fletcher!" She turned to look at him with a radiant smile. "You came!"

He emerged in between two collectors, looking absolutely dashing in his tux. Two women eyed him appraisingly, and Suki rushed toward him. "I said I would, didn't I?" He smiled back. "Or didn't you believe me?" He gave her a luscious kiss and turned to shake hands with Zeebo. "Well, hello there. How's your arm?"

"Better, much better," Zeebo answered, inspecting his arm for damages.

Suki excused herself from the group and ushered Fletcher over to a corner of the room.

"Where have you been? What happened? Did you catch Luchek?"

"Whoa, slow down. All in good time."

"But—" Her mind was racing with a thousand questions, and she barely knew where to begin. The last week had passed so quickly and so eventfully that she could hardly believe she was really here. She had left her showing in Vail with some hesitation, reluctant to leave her sculptures unattended, but there had been no choice. Then she had worked with Zeebo on a bio sketch and inventory of her work, and had arranged to fly the policeman to San Francisco, and had come to San Francisco herself only last night. In all that time, she hadn't heard from Fletcher. "Where've you been?" she asked, trying to sound casual.

"Just as busy as you," he answered. "When I'm working on a difficult case, I don't even have time to shave." He gave her a warm smile. "Besides, I knew I'd be seeing you here. That's worth a phone call, isn't it?"

She melted. "Yes. I've very glad to see you, I admit it. But—oh, go on, Fletcher, tell me what's been happening. You don't have to play detective with me any longer, do you? Just come out with it."

"Come on," he said, offering his arm. "People are filing in. We'd better get a front seat."

"But—"

"Later," he insisted, and she relented. She had learned by now not to try to pry information out of him. In any event, the auction was certainly enough of a distraction. She took a deep breath and took his proffered arm, trying to keep from trembling. "Why a front seat?" she asked nervously. "I think I'd rather hide in the back."

"You want to hear the bidding," Fletcher explained smoothly as he escorted her into the auction room, "but you don't want to see it. Since you're the artist, it would be too nerve-racking."

They took two seats off to the side up front and waited. The waiting was terrible. Zeebo found them and sat on Suki's left, taking her hand encouragingly.

"Don't be nervous, Suki," he said, "I already know that two of my clients are here for the sole purpose of purchasing your work." He glanced at Fletcher, businessman to businessman, and added, "I'd purchase it myself, but that would only slow Suki's career at this point by diminishing the value."

"Maybe I should have bought one last week in Vail," Fletcher said. "I know just which one—'Anticipation of a Kiss.'" He took Suki's hand and squeezed it.

"I had my eye on that one as well," Zeebo put in, unaware of Fletcher's meaning. "But, believe me, an auction is the only way. It's like a big free advertisement, telling the world that someone new has arrived."

The auctioneer's gavel struck the podium a few times, bringing the lively chatter in the room to a halt. The ensuing silence was tremendously agonizing for Suki. Now there was nothing to do but sit and wait, watching the works of other artists being auctioned before hers. It seemed to take forever as, one after another, each piece was brought up on the stage and exhibited for a brief moment while the auctioneer explained its worth. The bidders were mostly silent, which unnerved Suki the most, but Fletcher never let go of her hand.

"All those silent bids are driving me crazy," she whispered. "You never know who is bidding."

"That's part of the fun," Zeebo said. "Most people like to remain anonymous."

They watched as a painting was set up on the stage.

"That's a Kamarov, isn't it?" Fletcher asked with interest.

Suki sat up to look at it.

"It most certainly is," Zeebo said, eyeing the painting with knowledgeable anticipation. "He just defected last month, leaving all his other paintings behind in Russia. It was written up in *Time* this week."

The auctioneer concluded his comments and began the bidding. The opening of five hundred dollars rose steadily and quickly by five-hundred-dollar increments, until at last the price reached six thousand dollars.

"Six thousand dollars, going once, twice—" The gavel came down with a decisive bang. "Sold! For six thousand dollars."

"Oh, Lord," Suki groaned. "That was too fast for my blood. Couldn't you guys just knock me out and wake me when it's all over?" She shook her head. "And a little low for an original Kamarov, if you ask me. I wonder who the lucky collector is who bought that."

"Me," Zeebo said, smiling. He stood up and went over to claim the painting, leaving a deflated Suki clutching at Fletcher's arm.

"I'm so glad you're here," she said. "I couldn't get through this alone."

"Zeebo is here," Fletcher pointed out sensibly.

"That's not the same," Suki admitted, "and you know it."

Fletcher leaned down and kissed her swiftly, obliterating the auction for a brief moment. "That's for extra good luck," he whispered.

The auction continued with Suki holding Fletcher's hand so tightly at times that the blood seemed to stop. Four more times the gavel came down on final bids, until at last Suki's sculpture was carefully set up on the stage.

"Suzuki Lavette's 'Policeman,'" the auctioneer announced.

Suki listened numbly as her background was read. It was professional and to the point.

"I wrote that presentation personally," Zeebo told her. "I want the work to overshadow the artist. It's only appropriate, wouldn't you say?"

Suki was in no shape to answer. She gripped Fletcher's hand and he gave her a little squeeze. She felt an invisible connection with him, one that she was sure was not restricted to the tension of the auction. He cared about her. Not just her connection to the case and not even just her work, but her. It was now clear as sunlight. Her heart wanted to sing and shout with joy, but she was too terrified of what was going to happen in the next five minutes of her life. Everything went on hold as the auctioneer started to speak.

"We'll start the bidding at two hundred."

Suki's heart pounded madly as two hundred easily

rose to three, four, five, six, and then seven hundred dollars.

"Seven hundred going once—do I hear eight?"

"It's all so fast," Suki whispered, shaking.

"Going twice!" The auctioneer's gavel rose high, but it never hit the table. Instead, it pointed all the way to the back of the room as if he had been taken by surprise. "Eight hundred!"

Suki let out an excited breath, and even the unflappable Zeebo moved to the edge of his seat. Fletcher was listening alertly, still holding on to her hand.

"Nine hundred! One thousand! Eleven! Twelve! Thirteen . . . thirteen . . . do I hear fourteen? Fourteen?"

Surprisingly, Zeebo was the first to break. "I *must* know who the bidders are who want you so madly." He looked at Suki and Fletcher as if to apologize for breaking the unwritten rule of the auction. "For business purposes, it's allowed." He stood up and threw a cautious look toward the back.

"We have fourteen!" came the auctioneer's voice. "Fifteen! Sixteen! Sixteen," he repeated.

"Ahhh." Zeebo returned to his seat, satisfied. "Mr. Taylor, of course. He always bids by scratching his chin." Zeebo laughed at some private joke before continuing. "There's a new face. A very large man with a round, large frame. Wearing a leather jacket. Bids like an excited peasant at a country fair."

"Sixteen! Going once . . . Do I hear seventeen?"

"I can't look," Suki said, shutting her eyes. Fletcher said nothing, but he turned discreetly to look for the bidders.

"Going twice . . ."

Suddenly, Fletcher's hand jerked away from hers as if he had been hit by lightning. Suki opened her eyes and looked at him. He was staring fixedly at someone in the audience. A split second later he made a subtle motion with his hand.

"Seventeen!" The auctioneer's voice rose in excitement.

Suki couldn't believe her eyes. Even Zeebo was astonished.

"Am I crazy, or did you just bid?"

"Quiet," Fletcher said. "I don't want him to know I'm here bidding against him."

"You don't want who to know what?" Suki asked.

Fletcher ignored her question, calculating to himself. "Of course. What a fool I've been. It all makes sense." He seemed almost possessed. "And all the time, it was right under my nose."

"What was?" Suki looked at Zeebo, who shrugged.

"Seventeen," the auctioneer repeated. "Do I hear eighteen?"

Fletcher was still stunned. "So that's his scheme."

"Scheme?" Suki tried shaking his arm. *"Whose?"*

"Seventeen going once . . . twice . . ."

Suddenly a deep, resonant and all-too-familiar voice made a leap into the building. "Two thousand dollars."

"Oh, no, it can't be who I think it is." Suki froze, terrified. She couldn't believe her ears. She turned around and looked to the back of the auditorium, until her eyes fell on a familiar, unwelcome figure. "It's Luchek!"

Fletcher pulled her down. "Don't let him see you," he ordered tersely.

"We have two thousand, so I hear twenty-one hundred?"

Fletcher lifted his hand slightly, again catching the auctioneer's eye.

"We have twenty-one."

By now the room was filled with excitement.

"This is wonderful!" Zeebo said. "I couldn't have ordered better."

"Three thousand!" Luchek called out, stunning the crowd.

"What's going on?" Suki asked frantically. "Why is he here?" She pulled on Fletcher's sleeve, but he was concentrating intently. A second later, he held up four fingers, and waited for the auctioneer to recognize his bid.

"Four thousand," the auctioneer announced.

"Six thousand dollars," Luchek countered loudly, sending a buzz of energy through the audience.

The auctioneer looked for a call of seven, and glanced hopefully at Fletcher, who was still thinking carefully.

"So that's what he was doing in the exhibition hall that night." He looked up at the auctioneer, nodding once.

Suki became frightened. "What are you talking about?"

"The first night we were down setting up your sculptures and Luchek came in. He wasn't hiding himself, he was hiding the two million—in your sculpture."

Suki's eyes grew round with shock. She looked at Fletcher, expecting support, but he was concentrating with all his faculties on the auction. His eyes were razor-sharp, like an eagle going in for the kill.

"Eight thousand dollars." Luchek pronounced each word slowly, definitively.

By now Fletcher was ready to pounce. His face was tight and controlled. "I can't wait to see the look on his greedy face when he sees me."

Suki was tugging desperately at him. "Fletcher, listen to me. Please, don't do this."

"I have to. It's my job."

The auctioneer called for nine, and Fletcher waved inconspicuously.

"We have nine thousand."

The audience was humming with expectation, waiting to see how the show would end. But Luchek wasn't ready to end it. "Ten thousand," his baritone voice proclaimed without missing a beat.

And again the tide of reaction from the audience was followed by a bid of eleven thousand from Fletcher, which was immediately followed by twelve.

"This could go on forever," Fletcher realized aloud. "After all, what would you bid for two million dollars?"

Suki wanted to scream when he said that. Her most important moment was being destroyed. Her work should have been auctioned for its own worth, not for what had been hidden inside it by a crook. Now the auction had become a mockery, and he was contributing to the debacle. But she couldn't get Fletcher to listen to her. There was nothing that could interfere with his driven, intense concentration at that moment. He had ceased to the man she knew.

"Twelve thousand. Do I hear thirteen?"

"Please, Fletcher," she begged. "Stop and listen to me!"

He gave her a hard look. "Why should I? For all I know, you two were setting me up. And I was the perfect patsy."

That did it. She grabbed his lapels, trying to shake him. "Stop this right now!" Her face was desperate.

"Going once . . ." The auctioneer glanced at Fletcher."

Suddenly, there was a dead silence. He looked at her as if she had actually slapped him. "You're right. I will stop." He folded his arms and allowed the auctioneer to call a final count.

"Twelve thousand going twice . . ."

Suki's eyes were pinned on Fletcher. He wore a very satisfied look, as if he had just adopted a new plan, one that he was sure would work and that he was going to keep a secret.

Tears blurred her vision as she watched him. No one else, not even Zeebo, who knew nothing about Luchek, could understand or share her feeling of utter loss and humiliation. Only Fletcher could have consoled her, and he had abandoned her.

The auctioneer gazed at Fletcher expectantly, but there was no bid forthcoming. The gavel came down with one sharp bang, making Suki jump. "Sold to the gentleman in the back for twelve thousand dollars."

The audience applauded, and conversation rose around her as everyone eagerly discussed the new artist. Suki didn't want to hear it. Everything she had worked so hard for had gone up in smoke. She wanted no part of this sham.

But it wasn't over, not yet. As Luchek strutted to the front to pay for his new acquisition, Fletcher suddenly bolted up to the podium.

Suki wasn't sure who was most horrified, the audience, Luchek, or her. In the next instant, Fletcher picked up the auctioneer's gavel and held it menacingly over the sculpture. He looked at Luchek with a cold, triumphant smile.

"You're not getting away with the two million," he announced, and a second later, in front of a horrified group of people, a surprised thief, and the trembling artist, he smashed the sculpture right on its bottom.

Two guards grabbed him, but Fletcher was too strong for them, driven by his own purpose, and threw them off like flies. "Now watch this," he said, reaching inside the broken sculpture.

He groped around expectantly, but nothing happened. His face became impatient and then dismayed as he withdrew his hand. There was nothing in it. He looked accusingly at Luchek, who stared back at him, obviously just as stunned.

Luchek pushed past him angrily, with just a hint of fear in his face. He reached inside the statue himself, his hand moving frantically, but he, too, came up empty-handed.

"The money!" Luchek shouted.

Fletcher shook his head. "It's gone."

"It can't be," Luchek said. "I put it there myself. Who else could have taken it?"

The two men stood frozen on the stage, looking at each other and realizing the truth at the same instant. In unison, their eyes turned toward Suki.

"Oh, God, this can't be happening to me." Somehow she found her way to her feet, and began to run as if her life depended on it.

* * *

She was lying on the bed in her hotel room, in the same position she had taken four hours before, when Fletcher knocked abruptly on the door.

"Go away," she screamed.

"You're in big trouble, Suki."

"How dare you?" She glanced at the door angrily. "Leave me alone, Fletcher. Vamoose!"

Silence was followed by the all-too-familiar sound of her lock being worked by a bobby pin. She reached for the bottle of unopened champagne that lay in the watery ice bucket. Two glasses sat next to it on the side table. They had been intended for herself and Fletcher after the auction. She had left them there this morning, her spirits high and her future glittering ahead of her. All that seemed like a thousand years ago now.

When the door swung open, she saw Fletcher, still in his tuxedo, glaring at her. "It took me over four hours to locate you," was the first thing he said.

"One step farther and I'll clobber you—you Benedict Arnold."

He walked over calmly, calling her bluff. Suki was ready. If he'd thought she didn't mean it, he'd thought wrong. She lifted the bottle to bring it down on his head, but something stopped her at the last second.

He took the bottle from her trembling hand and examined the label. "Hmmm, Don Perignon," he said impressed. He spotted the two glasses, and instantly understood. "So, shall we celebrate your good fortune—and I do mean fortune?"

That statement made her glare heatedly at him, like a tigress about to pounce. He busied himself with opening the champagne, but Suki grabbed it out of his hand.

"I'll pour," she said icily, filling the two glasses. She held one up to her lips, took a sip, and smiled, as if enjoying the expensive wine. The other glass she held out invitingly for Fletcher to take. But when he reached for it, Suki threw its contents in his face.

He stood stunned and she nonchalantly placed the empty glass back down.

"This little act is quite clever," he said with murderous calm, producing a handkerchief and drying his face. "But don't think it has me fooled."

She remained silent.

"I've figured your entire game plan out. Would you like to hear it?"

Her silence prompted him to continue. "It's quite simple, really. You had me fooled from the very first day. Coincidences like yours just don't happen, they are made to happen." He watched Suki's eyes for signs of disturbance, but she remained reticent. "Here's how I see it. Luchek steals the money. He knows he may be followed, so he uses the old suitcase switch with an accomplice." He gestured grandly at her before continuing. "The deal is for you to smuggle the money out of Vail in your sculpture. That way, I go on a wild-goose chase following Luchek, while you head off in the opposite direction with the money."

At last Suki spoke. "Interesting theory," she said, pouring Fletcher another glass of champagne. She lifted it up and held it out to him. "Very interesting indeed, but I'm afraid you're all wet." With that she threw the second glass in his face, again placing it down near the bottle. "Care to go another round?"

He wiped his face readily, and continued undaunted. "It's unfortunate for Luchek that his lovely partner became greedy."

"By the way," Suki said nonchalantly. "Where is our friend Luchek?"

"At his hotel. He hasn't moved from there in four hours. The last I heard, he was hiring a detective to try to find you."

"I see. But now you've found me first." Suki sipped the champagne, feeling as if she needed needed it.

"Yes, I suppose I did." He pondered that for a moment, and then seemed to realize something of great importance. It was as though a magic wand had waved over him. Suki wasn't sure if he was just bluffing, but she was curious.

"Yes?" Suki asked. "Did you find a kink in your brilliant deductions?"

He gave a very surprised look. "Not a kink, but a new theory. It just came to me."

Suki refilled his glass and held it out of his reach. "Tell me what you're thinking."

Fletcher looked stunned. "Damn. If it's true—" He looked at her and shook his head. "But it can't be. If it were true, and you are innocent . . ."

"Be careful with your ifs," Suki warned him. "I'm still holding on to your glass. How do you want it? Straight up or with a twist?"

Fletcher was thinking very seriously, oblivious to her threats. Suki watched him, knowing she was still entranced by his intelligent energy but determined not to let it affect her.

"The policeman . . ." he murmured. "It had been damaged back in Vail . . ." His eyes gleamed as he probed closer to the truth. "But it looked brand-new at the auction." Suki nodded at his perceptiveness. "It was a great repair job."

"I'll give you a big clue," Suki said. "That is not the same statue as the one that was at the hotel in Vail. I made a new one last week from the same mold. I wasn't about to auction off damaged goods, you know."

"I knew it!" Fletcher exclaimed. "I knew I was right about that statue."

"And what were you wrong about?"

He looked at her radiantly. "Yes," he repeated. "You could be."

"Be what?"

"An innocent victim." He took a deep breath as he realized what this meant. "But if you are innocent . . ."

"If?"

Suddenly, he dropped onto the bed next to her, his face charged with urgency. "Suki, I've made a terrible mistake."

She let out a sigh. "How nice. So you finally see the light."

"Not just the light, but the whole picture. But if you aren't in on this theft, then the money is still in the old statue, the one that was damaged."

It was as if a shaft of sunlight had suddenly burst into her life, giving her a new ray of hope. "That's true," Suki admitted, her face changing. "I never realized it, but—oh, Fletcher . . ."

"The old statue, Suki." He took both her hands in his, beseeching her. "Where is it?"

"Oh, my God."

"The statue with the money in it. What did you do with it?"

Her hand covered her mouth, and she gazed at him, horrified. "I have one question."

"Ask it."

Suki closed her eyes and wondered how this could possibly be happening to her. When would this nightmare end? "When garbagemen collect trash," she whispered slowly, "do they throw it out in a big pile—or do they burn it?"

- 8 -

DURING THE ENTIRE PLANE RIDE to Denver, Fletcher continually badgered Suki with detailed questions about her garbage. When was it picked up, in what kind of vehicle, how many men, where was it dumped, and so forth.

To all these questions Suki could only venture a guess, but Fletcher was back on target, zeroing in for a kill, and he wasn't about to let up.

"I told you for the hundredth time," Suki said adamantly as they left the terminal and hailed a cab. "I do not know when they burn the garbage in Denver. I even had to find out from you that they do burn it, remember?"

"Smoke," Fletcher said. "Have you ever seen smoke coming from the sanitation department, and at what time?"

Suki sighed and ignored him as she got into the cab and gave the driver her address.

"You cabdrivers are pretty knowledgeable about the city you drive in," Fletcher said suddenly.

The driver shrugged philosophically.

Fletcher almost pounced on his new source of information. "When do they burn garbage in Denver?" he asked avidly.

The driver gave him a long, suspicious glance in the rearview mirror. "They sell tickets and wait till they've sold out," he said, and burst into raucous laughter.

Suki laughed with him, but Fletcher wasn't interested in jokes. He was all business.

"You are a sad case," Suki said to him as they made their way into Denver. The evening sky sported a full moon, and it bathed the surrounding mountains in ghostly light. "I'm supposed to be back at the hotel in Vail," she fretted. "My sculptures are still on exhibit there, you know."

"Just bear with me," he said. "We could be almost finished with this mess. Then I'll fly with you to Vail and help you pack those sculptures myself. Is it a deal?"

All Suki could do was sigh. Everything had become tangled in a hopeless knot. She wasn't sure she wanted Fletcher's company all the way to Vail—not if he was going to be obsessed with the case the whole time. She still hadn't recovered from the shock of the auction, but all he could think about was the case.

When at last they pulled up in front of Suki's apartment, which was situated on the parlor floor of a large Victorian house, Fletcher jumped out excitedly. "Do you have a car?" he asked Suki.

"Uh—well, no. I did, but it died. Budding artists aren't big on cars, you know. Too expensive to maintain."

Fletcher produced a fifty-dollar bill from his pocket, ripped it in half, and gave a piece to the driver. "Wait here."

The driver took the bill and gave a sardonic laugh. "Gee, thanks, a twenty-five dollar tip."

"You'll get the other half later," Fletcher told him. "Just be sure and wait for us." The cabdriver brightened considerably.

Suki shook her head. Fletcher was overdoing it. He stood on the curb, waiting impatiently as the driver stepped out to sit on the stoop.

"What's his problem?" the cabby asked her.

Suki shrugged, controlling her annoyance. "He lost two million dollars, and he thinks that's the end of the world."

The cabdriver did a double take.

Fletcher was already rummaging through the garbage cans. He picked one up and dumped the contents onto the sidewalk. "You said you put the cop down here in pieces, right?"

"I broke off the arms and legs from the torso and put it in a couple of cans. It was too hard to fit it all in one," she explained.

The cabdriver leaped up and stared at them wildly. "*What?* Listen, folks I don't think I like the sound of this."

Suki waved away his trepidation. "We're talking about a broken sculpture," she explained hurriedly, "not a real body."

"Oh." The driver sank back down, watching them suspiciously.

Fletcher dropped the can and frowned. "Does this look like the same garbage you left here?"

Suki came over and surveyed the mess wearily. "It was seven in the morning," she said. "I didn't really examine the garbage." She bent down and began picking up the mess he had just made.

"I'll bet they picked it up already," he deduced. "We'll have to head over to the city dump. I only hope it's still there." He walked purposefully back to the cab, Suki trotting after him.

The Denver Department of Sanitation was located on a beautiful, hilly road. As they drove along, Suki reacquainted herself with Colorado's beauty in the moonlight, but Fletcher wasn't looking at the scenery.

"At least it's a full moon," he surmised. "It will make it easier to see what we're doing."

"And what is it we'll be doing exactly?"

The driver knew the answer to that one. "We'll be looking for two million bucks, right?" he asked eagerly, having got into the spirit of the evening.

At the entrance to the city dump, Fletcher explained to the guard at the gate what he needed. "It's a torso, a plastic mannequin that looks exactly like the body of a policeman."

The guard scratched his head and took a sip of lukewarm coffee in a Styrofoam cup. "You can try, but if it isn't burned, it's over there in that heap." He pointed to a small mountain in the yard near the incinerator. It was an Everest of garbage.

Suki moaned at the sight. "It will take us a whole day to weed through all that."

"Enjoy yourself," the guard said. "What's so important about it, anyway.

"Two million dollars in cash," the cabdriver announced importantly.

Before five minutes had elapsed, over thirty sanitation workers who had formerly been lolling around, watching the clock and looking busy when the supervisor appeared, materialized out of nowhere. Unfortunately, none of them remembered picking up a mannequin of a cop. Fletcher persuaded them to call everyone on the day shift, promising a big reward, but nothing turned up. The sculpture must have been incinerated. Suki sighed. The thought of all that money going up in smoke was crushing.

She knew the case would be over if the money were gone, and she wanted Fletcher to be victorious. Not only that, but her tenuous involvement with him would continue only as long as there was a case to solve. She equated losing the case with losing Fletcher, realizing somberly how much he had come to mean to her.

After a good hour of searching, Fletcher and Suki were both a mess. Her hands were frozen, her face was grimy, and her clothes were torn. Fletcher wasn't faring any better.

She walked over to him slowly, removed some shreds of newspaper from his coat, and tapped him gently on the shoulder. He turned, dejected. "Well, at least Luchek didn't get it."

Suki put her hands on his arms sympathetically. "At least you don't suspect me anymore."

He looked at her and summoned a bittersweet smile. "I'm sorry I put you through all this."

Suki chanced a smile back. "Well, it has been—exciting."

"I destroyed your sculpture," he reminded her bluntly.

"It can be fixed. And I can always make another sculpture. I still have the original mold, you know." She smiled encouragingly, and Fletcher nodded.

"At least Luchek doesn't have the money," he said. "Now that would be depressing. At least this way, no one will have it."

"How about going back to my place and getting cleaned up? I'll fix you my specialty," she added sympathetically when she saw the defeat in his eyes.

"Thanks." He bent and kissed her briefly, and she clung to him, knowing that he needed her support.

"Let's go," she whispered.

Just then a man called out near the edge of the incinerator building. Everyone stopped their rummaging and turned to look. He was standing knee-deep in garbage that was about to head into the furnace. As he was silhouetted against the light from the inside of the building, they could see that he was holding a mannequin's arm. In the hand attached to the arm was a gun.

"That's it!" Suki cried, breaking loose from Fletcher and running over. Fletcher was right behind her.

Suki waded through the debris until she reached the man. She took the plastic arm and held it up to the light. But her happiness was short-lived.

"Sorry, folks, but I'm afraid this is all that remains of your mannequin," the man said, shaking his head. He pointed down over the closed safety gate to the fiery light inside. "The rest of that statue is down there. It must have been shoveled in with the last batch a few minutes before you got here."

They all looked down in helpless frustration at the blazing fire, which almost seemed to be mocking them.

But Fletcher refused to give up, and several of the men agreed with his tenacity. Two million dollars was worth fighting for. The place turned to pandemonium as everybody gathered in the one spot and began diving through the garbage, hoping against hope. It was as if their very lives depended on it. After fifteen minutes of lunacy, the pile had been reduced to scattered rubble.

"It's no use," Fletcher said, throwing his arms up in despair. "Thanks, fellows, but let's forget it." He went over to the safety gate and looked down through the grating at the fire below. His face was set grimly, his mouth compressed in a hard little line. Suki came and stood next to him.

"It's the first time I've ever failed," he explained slowly. "And my poor client is going to have to declare bankruptcy."

Suki put her hand on his shoulder, but he moved away from her, and banged his fist hard on the gate.

"Damn! A perfect record shot."

Suki tried another approach. "You gave it your best, Fletcher. No one can win all the time."

He spoke bitterly. "Well, my best wasn't good enough." He turned and looked at her, and it jolted her to see that some of the fire had gone out of his eyes, the crystal-blue eyes that she had seen alive with energy. "I was so close! That day we met, I had that money right in my hand, and the culprit within reach." He made a wild gesture of impatience and let his fist bang down on the gate once again.

"That was my fault, too," Suki said quietly. "I guess I should have trusted you more."

He looked at her and shook his head. "How could you? I was too busy not trusting you."

There was a pause. Suki put her hand back on his shoulder. "I think distrust has been our biggest enemy here, not Luchek."

Fletcher let out a hard chuckle. "To think that all my detective life, trust was the one thing I could never afford. Now I find out that it's the one thing I should have learned to have. You've got to trust someone, or you end up going around in circles." He surprised her by suddenly taking her in his arms and kissing her gently on the forehead. "Can you accept an apology from an overzealous nut?"

Suki gazed up at him, stunned. "You mean you don't think I was involved with Luchek?"

"No," he said simply.

"But how can you know that?" She grimaced. "Hell, even I can see that the facts still point to me."

He looked at her and smiled mysteriously. "I just know. Call it instinct."

"Instinct?" Suki was doubtful but happy at the same time. "Well, how do you explain my having the same luggage as Luchek?"

"Coincidence," Fletcher said easily. "Besides, after I left Vail last week, I began noticing that damn suitcase every time I was at an airport. And believe me, in the past week I've been through a lot of airports."

"What about the ten thousand dollars in my purse?" she pressed, determined to have this out.

"In your haste, you forgot it was there. Besides, why would Luchek tie you up if you were working with him?"

"For appearances," Suki found herself saying. She was certainly giving him every opportunity to doubt her word, but she wanted it that way. She was sick of wanting him and having to prove herself to him at the same time. If he could believe her now, she'd know that he meant it. "I could have had him do that in order to fool you." She spoke patly, testing him. "Face it, Fletcher, there is no logical reason for you to trust me."

"Then you'll have to settle for an illogical one. Look, Suki, I just got defeated on a very big case. I should be utterly miserable, and yet one very good thing came out of all this."

"What?" she asked innocently.

He grabbed her and held her so tightly that she couldn't breathe for a second. Then he kissed her with a masterful ardor that left her limp. The kiss would have lasted forever, but the cabdriver began to clear his throat loudly.

"Uh, sorry to break up this little tryst, folks, but . . ." He waved the torn bill at Fletcher. "I'd like to earn the other half of this today, if you don't mind?"

They broke away reluctantly, but sat cuddled together like two teenagers in the back of the cab. Fletcher was holding on to her as if he would never let her go, kissing her often and letting his hands steal under her coat to hold her even more closely. Suki knew that he wanted her, but that his desire was tempered by his sharp disappointment at losing his case. She took his hand and squeezed it, her heart swelling.

"Well, it's sure been interesting," the driver remarked as they pulled to a stop in front of Suki's house. He turned around expectantly, and Fletcher fished in his pocket, pulling out the other half of the fifty-dollar bill.

"Here you go," he said briefly, handing it to the cabby. "Thanks for everything."

They got out of the cab and waited while the driver took Suki's famous suitcase from the trunk, letting it land on the pavement with a decisive thud.

"He must think we're crazy," Suki observed as the cab tore off.

"We are," Fletcher said.

Hand in hand, they ran up the steps, lugging the suitcase, when suddenly Suki burst into a fit of giggles. It was all so ridiculous. Here they were, dragging a crazy-looking suitcase that had caused an unbelievable heap of trouble. She had actually been a suspect in a very serious crime, and she had managed to fall for the man who suspected her. She glanced at Fletcher, afraid he would be hurt by her laughter, but he was smiling at her, understanding her reaction. His face twitched suddenly, and then he was laughing, too, some of his bitterness dispelled by the utter ludicrousness of their present circumstance.

"Look at us! We're a mess!" he exclaimed, leaning against the door as she fished for her key.

"Well, here we are," Suki said, shaking her head as she opened the door. She flicked on the light, shrugged out of her coat, and reached out automatically to drop it on the wooden coatrack next to the door. But her hands weren't steady, and the coat missed the rack, dropping to the floor. "Whoops!" She laughed. breathlessly. "That's the first time that's ever happened."

Fletcher picked up the coat and deposited it on a wooden arm, studying the coatrack curiously. It was an elaborate, carved contraption, but it fit into the two-room apartment that had retained the original woodwork and chandeliers. The place was filled with Suki's experiments and paintings, the most interesting of which was a startlingly real sculpture of a man with a cane.

Suki went over to it and turned it so that it faced the window. "People do a double take when they walk by my house and see him in the window,'' she explained. "Boy, this place is a mess," she muttered. "I don't remember leaving it like this."

"Never mind that. I wanted to see how and where you lived," Fletcher said, examining a painting of a butterfly. He walked around curiously, looking at all the knickknacks and mementos that were displayed in places of honor in between the comfortable furniture. "It's very . . . you."

"Well—yes. Thank you. If that was a compliment."

"Oh, it was." His eyes turned into two liquid pools, melting her with their warmth. Suki stared back at him, her heart jumping ahead.

"You know what we need?" he said suddenly.

"What?"

"A bath!"

She giggled again and nodded wordlessly, wondering what he would do next.

She didn't have long to wait. He found the bathroom on the other side of the tiny kitchen and instantly turned on the water to fill up the tub. As he came back out, she saw that he had taken a new attitude, and her heart lifted. He gallantly offered her an arm, summoning all of his charm. "Care to join me, madam?"

Suki hesitated for only a split second. Then she sailed across the room as gracefully as a princess and took the outstretched arm, her eyes shining into his.

Together, they entered the old-fashioned Victorian bathroom, tiled in black and white and featuring an enormous porcelain tub that sat on four lion's feet. Already, mounds of frothy bubbles were floating on the water.

"Shall we?" he asked graciously, reaching at once for the buttons of her shirt. His elegant tone belied the swift sensuality of his gestures, and the combination was wildly arousing. His fingers flew down the front of her shirt, pausing for only a second to admire her breasts when they appeared. Everything was forgotten now—Luchek, the money, the case, the suspicions that had nagged at both of them since they had met. Now there was only this moment, and Suki knew with certainty that Fletcher intended to enjoy it as much as she did.

All the tensions and doubts that had built up exploded in a mist of passion as he unclasped her bra and let it fall to the floor. She was helping him now, opening her jeans and stepping out of them. His eyes feasted hungrily on her body before his hands moved to his own clothing.

"No, wait," she said huskily. "Let me." He stood still, watching her intently as she slowly, tantalizingly, revealed his body to her curious, hungry eyes. He was as lean and powerful as she had thought, but with a bronzed elegance that nearly took her breath away. He stepped back, his arousal evident not only in the response of his body but in the fire that raged in his eyes.

He reached down and turned off the water. The mountains of bubbles floated gently, waiting for them. He stepped in first, submerging his body with a long, appreciative "ahhh." Suki followed, stepping in to face him, reveling in the delicate tease of the bubbles against her skin.

They played at first like two children, but with a sly undercurrent that spoke of what was to come. First Suki lifted a cloud of bubbles in one hand and blew it gently toward Fletcher. The cloud landed on his shoulder, dissolving slowly as it slid down his chest. Then Fletcher lifted mounds of bubbles in both hands and placed them directly on Suki's breasts, massaging gently. Her nipples rose to taut peaks and she closed her eyes, letting him wash her and possess her as her breathing sharpened.

Her hands floated freely in the water, and soon she lifted more bubbles and applied them to Fletcher's shoulders, massaging and cleansing him as he had done to her. Her fingers lingered for teasing moments on the tight male nipples, bringing them to hard knots, and then moved on again, covering his chest with long, relishing strokes. Fletcher's head fell back, and he groaned, which thrilled her as much as any touch. The masterful Fletcher Colman, always in perfect control, was now under her spell, and she gloried in her conquest.

Not that she wasn't being conquered as well. Fletcher's hands worked magic on her body, arousing and then withdrawing, bringing incoherent syllables from her lips as she sank deeper and deeper into the pleasure. Never had she felt so carefree and so bold, offering her body as naturally as if their union had been planned and sanctioned a thousand years before. This moment was only the crowning pinnacle of that plan.

Their eyes met during a brief, timeless juncture, and Fletcher smiled. "I think we're clean now," he murmured.

She nodded wordlessly, lifting a bubbly arm to the side of the tub. They emerged together, two slippery bodies dripping suds that ran between their legs and fell into dissolving mounds on the floor. They shared one huge towel, drying only perfunctorily before dashing to the huge Victorian brass bed that was covered with an ivory eyelet spread.

Suki lay back slowly, reaching her arms out to him. They fell back together, kissing again and again, leaving heated trails of kisses on each other's faces and throats and shoulders. Fletcher made impulsive sounds of appreciation as he explored her slender, still-damp body, bringing her breasts to fullness and finding the warm hollow between her thighs. The moment he touched it, her back arched involuntarily. His eyes lit with seductive pleasure, and he continued his slow, feathery ministrations, murmuring of her beauty and her passion as he aroused her.

He brought her to the teetering edge and drew back, letting her find him as he had found her. She touched him tentatively at first, and then with gathering heat and confidence as he shuddered deliciously in response. Faster and bolder, her strokes grew, until he was straining against her and her body opened effortlessly for him, easing back and uniting with his in a liquid rush of pleasure.

Now they were truly together, seeking and finding each new rhythm, clasping each other for dear life, hurtled forward and upward on a single course that knew only one end. How easy this was, Suki thought dreamily as they crested the waves. How easy and how right. Fletcher seemed to know exactly what she was thinking and confirmed it with every subtle motion of his body. She did not quite understand how she could know this, but mere words had become commonplace and meaningless. The magical connection between their bodies told her everything she needed to know.

In a timeless moment, they entered a radiant sunburst of sensation, stars and rockets exploding around them as they clung together. And then, with slow, languid moans of release, they drifted back down through the clouds, letting themselves settle wherever the mood took them.

When Suki ventured to open her eyes a small eternity later, she found that they were still on her bed in her apartment in Denver, not in some ethereal kingdom in the clouds. Her eyelids fluttered lazily, but when she caught sight of Fletcher looking at her, she managed a lopsided smile.

"Hi." He smiled at her.

"Hi yourself."

They looked deeply into each other's eyes for another timeless span, letting the minutes or hours or whatever they were drift harmlessly by. But at length another sensation made itself known, demanding her attention. Hunger, that was it. She groped awkwardly toward the nightstand, reaching for her clock. It wasn't there.

Twisting around reluctantly, she examined the nightstand. The small digital clock that she always kept by the edge of the stand was now facing the wall.

"I am getting clumsy," she said as she turned it around and brought it back to its usual position. "It's nine-thirty," she announced. "Would you like something to eat?"

"Okay. Would you like to go out?"

She shook her head. "No, not now. I'm going to fix a snack, and then I'm going to sketch you." She reached under her bed for her pad and drawing pencil, but they weren't there. "Just a second," she said, flipping over the side to have a look down under. The pad and charcoals had moved all the way across the floor. "That's odd," she said.

"What is?"

She looked slowly around the room. "Ever since we got here, I've had the strangest feeling that things aren't right. It's as if everything had been moved just a fraction of an inch. Nothing is missing or out of place exactly—just a little off."

Fletcher sat bolt upright, instantly on guard. "You've been searched," he said excitedly.

"Searched?" she repeated, frightened. "You mean —someone was in here?"

"It certainly appears that way." He sounded anything but alarmed, and she regarded him with horror, falling back on the bed.

"Oh, Lord," she groaned. "What next?"

He tugged at her arm. "Don't you get it, Suki? Someone was here looking for the sculpture."

"But I threw it out," she said impatiently.

"I know, I know. But maybe he got to it before we did."

"I thought you said Luchek was in San Francisco with us. How could he be in two places at once?"

He had a ready answer. "An accomplice. It has to be." He grabbed her and sat her up, her hair spilling over her breasts. "The money may be in Luchek's possession right now!" He was so excited that he could barely contain himself.

Suki shook her head and looked at him with grave doubt. "I don't understand you at all, Fletcher. Back at the dump, you were glad that at least the money wasn't in Luchek's hands. Now you seem thrilled that it could be."

"At least there's a chance that it isn't burned." he explained. "At least it's somewhere. Somewhere where it can be found." His eyes turned to hard glints. "And if it can be found, you'd better believe I'm going to find it." Without another word, he leaped out of bed and ran into the bathroom, retrieving his clothes.

Suki sat silently in the bed, watching him. Everything had happened so quickly. This man had become her lover, and now he was tearing out in such a hurry that the magic they had made hung tenuously, in danger of perishing. She felt naked and vulnerable, about to lose something that had only just become precious to her.

"Give me a call from Zanzibar," she said wryly as he covered not only his body, but also the lovely openness that had been hers only minutes before. She tried to sound jaunty, but she couldn't disguise the wistful sadness in her voice.

He came to her, his eyes begging forgiveness. "Please, Suki. This case is almost over. I have to go, don't you see that?"

She nodded dully. "It's just that you're always leaving, always running out. At very crucial moments, I might add."

He smiled ruefully. "I admit, the timing has been rotten. But bear with me, will you? It's not always like this, I swear." Bending down, he kissed her with a piercing sweetness that made his departure all the more unbearable. "I'll call you," he murmured, nuzzling her hair for a tender moment.

Suki didn't bother telling him that this was the line that had kept women on the string since the invention of the telephone. She threw her arms around his neck and kissed him one last time. "Take care of yourself," she whispered. "And I do mean that."

"I will," he promised with a wink. He left quietly, closing the door with only a little click to break the silence.

- 9 -

SUKI KNELT ON THE FLOOR of the exhibition hall in Vail a week later, sealing the last crate into which she had just packed the final sculpture, "Anticipation of a Kiss."

Fletcher Colman had not made an appearance during the past week, although she had received one cryptic message from him on her answering machine. "Hi, it's Fletcher, Thursday at noon. I'll be at area code 312, 555-0080 for the next hour. From four to five I'll be at area code 612, 555-1819. Try and get back to me." She had received this message the next day, too late to answer it, although she had tried to call him at both numbers anyway. No one had answered.

Knowing Fletcher had certainly been interesting, she reflected as she headed to the main desk to leave detailed shipping instructions. The man might be aggravating, but at least he was never dull. The memory of what it had been like to lie in his arms continued to haunt her, surprising her with its strength late at night, when she was most vulnerable. She tried to tell herself not to count on Fletcher, that he would leave her life as quickly as he had entered it, but it was no use. The flickerings of love had already started burning in her heart, and she knew that seeing him again, under any circumstance at all, would only fan the flames. *I'm in for it,* she thought as she took the elevator back up to her room.

She flung the door open, determined to take a hot shower and put Fletcher Colman out of her mind. But when she walked inside, there was Fletcher in person, stretched out comfortably on her bed.

"Hi," he said cordially, waving a friendly hello.

"Fletcher!" Suki gripped the doorknob to steady herself. She should be used to his surprises by now, but nothing would ever accustom her to the gladness that electrified her whenever she saw him. And he certainly had a disconcerting habit of popping up in unlikely places. "What are you doing here?"

He grinned. "I just stopped by for a visit."

"You just—" She staggered inside and collapsed on the bed. "Are you as exhausted as I am?"

"Probably. I've been all over the country following leads on Luchek.

She looked at him lounging on her bed and had the sudden, irreverent thought that she should tear off her clothes and jump into bed with him. But curiosity conquered passion, at least for now. Too much was at stake. "What did you find out?" she asked.

"A lot." Fletcher sat up and smiled, leaning over her with masterful grace. He reached out and caught a lock of silky black hair between his fingers. "It seems Luchek's pulled this sort of thing before. He's been a confidence man for years, and he finally turned his interests to the rock-concert business. He handled another concert last year in Chicago, where he absconded with all the cash from the ticket sales. Somehow he managed to launder all the money he stole with no problem."

"Launder?" Suki looked at him, perplexed. "What do you mean?"

"You just can't show up with two million dollars at a bank and try to open up an account," he explained. "You have to show where you got the money. In short, you have to prove you came by the money legally."

"I'll take your word for it," she said wearily. She didn't want to hear any more about stolen money and front men and laundering. She wanted to nestle into his arms and stay there.

Apparently, Fletcher had the same thought, because suddenly he was pulling her on top of him. She sprawled over him, delighted, her hair spilling onto his face.

"I was wondering if you were busy next week," he asked calmly, as if he always asked to see her under normal, average circumstances.

"Why?" she teased. "What did you have in mind?"

"Oh, a week in Mexico. How does that sound to you? I want to get away from all this snow."

"A simple week in Mexico, huh?" The man had style. She had to give him that. "I don't know," she said, pretending to hesitate. "My bobsled lessons start next week, and if you miss the first week they don't let you make it up."

He kissed her, silencing what remained of her protest, and sending her into a spinning circle of sensation. "So what do you say?" he asked, dropping tiny, tantalizing kisses down her neck. "Does Acapulco sound good?"

"You're serious about this, aren't you?" she asked, her eyes closed as she savored his touch. Suddenly, a week seemed much too long to have been away from him. His hands were addictive, she realized dreamily. And not just his hands, but all of him.

He smiled. "Why not?"

She turned sideways and cradled her body against his, resting her head on his shoulder. "But what about Luchek? Did you find out anything else?"

"Can I tell you later?" His voice had become husky as his hands drew dizzy designs up and down the length of her body.

"Oh, please, Fletcher. Just give me the basics."

Fletcher contented himself with exploring every female nook and cranny of her form as he ran down the events of the last week. He had followed up every lead and every clue that would put him within reach of Luchek, but so far the target himself had not materialized.

"What about his accomplice?" Suki asked, squirming as Fletcher's hand stole between her thighs.

"As far as I could ascertain, it has to be someone in the music business." The hand moved up her torso to her breast, finding its outline and tracing it delicately. "I'm still working on that angle. In the last week, I've been to record companies, rock concerts, and recording studios all over the country."

Suki sat up, impressed. "You certainly go beyond the call of duty, don't you?"

He threw his hands up. "I don't have much choice."

She frowned, considering. "I have the feeling that this is one of those things where the answer is right under your nose."

He laughed. "In that case, I must have a very long nose." She laughed with him, and he checked his watch. "You know what?"

"What?" she asked slyly.

"I'm starving."

She looked disappointed. "Oh."

Fletcher chuckled. "I've been traveling all day. I was thinking of terms of a long, leisurely dinner, a long, leisurely bath, a cordial or two, and then . . . who knows?" He grinned. "Now that doesn't sound so bad, does it?"

She couldn't help grinning back. "No, I guess not."

They rode down in the elevator holding hands, Suki's senses charged with anticipation of the evening ahead of her. Emerging from the elevator, they walked into the lobby and turned down the hall to the dining room, almost bumping into three odd-looking characters whom Suki immediately recognized.

"Suki Lavette, isn't it?" one of them said, his British accent confirming his identity. "You're that artist chick with the copper we bashed. Remember us?"

Suki smiled politely. "How could I forget—I mean, you broke my sculpture." They gaped back at her and she felt compelled to say something. "So—uh, how was your concert, Slime?"

"No, I'm Mud, this here's Grease, and that's Ooze. Slime's at the concert hall with our manager. And our concert is tonight."

"Oh, I'm sorry, I must have forgotten. I've been so busy, and—" She groped for a graceful way out of this conversation. "Oh, uh—Fletcher Colman, this is the Purple Sludge."

Fletcher extended a hand. "Oh, yes, you have that new song out, 'Hit Me Over the Head With a Tire Iron, Baby.' It's certainly—interesting. It really hits home."

Suki very much wanted to end this conversation. "Good luck on your concert tonight. I hope you get a big turnout."

"Oh, we will," Mud said proudly.

"We're sold-out," Ooze added.

"That's right, miss, we have a packed house."

Fletcher couldn't hide his astonishment. "Sold out? You guys are sold-out? I can't believe it. I mean—" He stopped abruptly, not wanting to be blatantly rude. "Uh, what I meant was—that's terrific news."

Suki gave him a relieved look after they were out of earshot. "Thank goodness we got out of that."

He laughed. "You're not kidding. It's funny, I've been so involved in the rock-music business lately that I actually knew who they were." A frown creased his face. "But it *is* awfully strange that they're sold-out."

"Why? Is it so hard to get people to go to a rock concert?" Suki shrugged.

"When it's given by the worst rock group in the

history of music it is. According to *Rolling Stone*, the Purple Sludge is the worst group ever to invade America from England. And I quote: 'They did not invade America. They were simply deported here.'"

Fletcher laughed. "I'd like to meet that manager of theirs. I'll bet he's either tone-deaf or stuffs his ears with cotton."

"Or with twenty-dollar bills," Suki said, stopping suddenly. She felt as if she'd just been struck by lightning.

"What is it, Suki?"

"I just remembered who their manager is." She thought back to that very first day when Slime had broken her policeman. "Yes, it all makes sense," she said with rising excitement. "That's why Luchek came to Vail."

He was listening avidly. *"Why?"*

"Because he's their manager!" she answered, almost shouting.

Fletcher gripped her arm. *"What?* How do you know that? Who told you?"

"Slime," she answered eagerly, her eyes shining with excitement. "The first day I was here." She rapidly told him what had happened that day, and his face lit up with the intensity of pursuit.

"So he came here to launder the money," he said, nodding avidly as he put the pieces together.

Suki turned to him. "But what do they do with all the cash from the sale of concert tickets?"

Fletcher laughed. "That's easy. They simply put it in the bank. It's the perfect cover."

"Wow," she said, awed. "It really is the perfect crime—only they don't know about us." She lifted a finger and pointed it back and forth between them.

He took the outstretched hand in his and kissed it. "You are brilliant, you know that?"

She looked up at him and smiled radiantly. "Thank you, sir. It looks like you and I are going to the Purple Sludge concert tonight."

His face compressed rapidly into a frown. "We are? How? It's sold-out, remember?"

She opened her purse and produced the two tickets that Slime had given her on the day he broke her statue. "My treat."

He examined the tickets with distaste. "You'll have to tell me why I'm going to the concert. Otherwise you couldn't get me to set foot inside that concert hall with all those screaming kids and their crazy getups."

"Good point," she noted, nodding thoughtfully. "We'll stick out like a sore thumb in these clothes. We'll need a disguise." She strode ahead, her mind working feverishly, and Fletcher came running after her.

"What do you mean? I'm certainly not going to dress up in any kind of disguise. Especially if it's the kind of disguise I think you're thinking about."

"Are you sure?" She stopped and looked back at him, her eyes twinkling.

That evening found them making their way along a trail near the base of the mountain that led to the huge concert hall. The temperature was around zero, and a stiff wind made it feel like thirty below. But what made it really outlandish was the clothes they were wearing.

Both of them had assembled punk outfits so that they would fit into the crowd and be able to move freely without being recognized. Suki was in skin-tight black leather with chains around her neck and purple suede boots. She had sprayed purple down the sides of her hair, which had all been combed to one side of her face and then teased mercilessly, so that it resembled a one-sided porcupine. Paper clips were attached to each ear, and she had used the most outrageous makeup she could find—white lipstick, purple eyeliner, blue mascara, and hot-pink blush. Fletcher was wearing newly purchased leopard-print jeans and a tiger-striped shirt, and his hair had been treated with mousse, teased up, and sprayed electric blue in the front.

He looked at her morosely and shivered. "It's freezing out here. We'll be blue before we get there."

"Don't worry, your hair already has a head start," she punned, hoping to make him laugh. Instead all she got was a dirty look. "I hope Luchek won't recognize us after all the trouble we took," she added.

"I wouldn't recognize you in broad daylight." He put his arm around her, pulling her close to keep both of them warm. Then he surprised her by kissing her soundly. "That's for being so perceptive," he said. "Even I didn't know Luchek was the Purple Sludge's manager. If your theory is right, and I know it will be, the only thing to expect at that concert is a lot of empty seats, Luchek, and two million dollars."

Suki shook her head. "It's amazing, isn't it? Luchek then claims he made that two million in cash by selling out the concert, and no one questions him because they don't know the truth. It's the perfect crime."

"It was."

Shivering, they arrived at the entrance with about five minutes to spare before the concert would begin. Sure enough, there was Donald Luchek himself, standing at the entrance and taking the tickets. Fletcher squeezed Suki's hand, and she ordered her heart to keep from thumping. A handful of teenagers ambled in, and Suki and Fletcher snapped their gum and turned their faces as if to look at the meager crowd. Fletcher handed both tickets to Luchek, who took them without glancing twice at them. They strolled into the auditorium, feeling as if they had just made it over the border from a war-torn country into freedom.

The auditorium was dark, but it was easy to see that only a handful of seats were taken. "Just as I thought," Suki said proudly, her confidence mounting by the minute.

Fletcher took her by the arm. "Come on. Don't get too proud of yourself, it makes you drop your guard. We've got to get backstage. I'm positive we'll find the money there."

They found their way backstage through a side door, narrowly missing one of the Purple Sludge, who was coming out of an office down the hall.

"That's Slime," Suki whispered.

They watched as Slime locked the door behind him.

"Hey, Slime!" It was Ooze calling to him. "Where you been, mate? We've been looking for you. You missed too many rehearsals already, and we don't want you to miss our concert, now do we? Let's go."

They left, and Fletcher and Suki headed straight for the office door. He took out his trusty bobby pin and worked on the lock.

"So," Fletcher said, skillfully twisting. "Our friend Slime has been missing rehearsals, has he?"

"Do you think he's mixed up in this?" Suki asked

incredulously as the door opened without a sound. "Boy, you're good."

He bowed gallantly. "At your service, madam." They made their way inside, flicked on the light, and closed the door.

"I think there's a good chance he was the one who searched your place and went to the dump for the money." His eyes darted around the room, landing triumphantly on two burlap money bags labeled "Sludge Concert Proceeds." "Aha! Care to guess what we'll find in those bags?"

"Nothing that should concern you," Luchek's voice interrupted them.

They turned and froze. He was standing in the doorway leveling a gun at them.

Slime came in after him and quickly locked the door. Suki's heart sank.

"I knew I'd find you two back here," Luchek said nastily. He looked them up and down and smiled. "Nice threads. You fit right in." He smirked. "I've heard of detectives using disguises, but this is ridiculous."

"The clothes you're going to be wearing soon come in one color only—prison blue," Fletcher retorted.

"Highly unlikely," Luchek said. "I'm not really planning to stay long in this country."

"Don't be so sure. I'll have you know I called the police before coming here."

Luchek chuckled. "Now, now, Mr. Colman. Let's not go through that routine again, please."

Suki was staring at Slime. "So, Slime, *you're* his accomplice," she stated.

Slime grinned in affirmation.

"What an appropriate name for you," Fletcher said cordially. "Tell me, is Slime your real name?"

"What difference will that make to you?" Luchek barked. "Suffice it to say that Slime has been an efficient associate in my little caper. And quite clever. It was his idea to hide the money in your sculpture," he said to Suki.

Slime nodded happily, quite pleased with himself. Suki realized that Fletcher's baiting of the two crooks was deliberate, that he wanted them to keep on talking, to keep revealing information while he thought of a way out of this mess. "Sorry that I bashed your copper and all," Slime said. "But this here detective was right on our backs. We had to find a way of smuggling the money out of Vail without it being noticed."

Suki shook her head as if scolding a child, and tried to think of something leading to say. "So you broke my sculpture on purpose that first day? Just to make a hole large enough to stuff in all that money?"

Slime nodded proudly, and Fletcher picked up the flow. "Once it was broken," he explained in a very interested tone, "they figured you'd try to fix it. Luchek undid the broken part in the gallery that night, stuffed the money inside, and repaired it himself on the spot. He figured you wouldn't notice the difference."

"Ahhh, but I did," Suki told him. "That's why I had to make a new sculpture."

Luchek laughed coldly. "What difference does it make now? I have the money."

"We have the money," Slime put in. "But right now I'm late. I've got a bloody rotten concert to give." He turned to leave. "Keep an eye on them. I'll meet you after the show."

Slime slammed the door, and Luchek laughed as he watched him go. "That stupid little punk." He looked at Suki and Fletcher and smiled. They didn't smile back. "He really believes that I'll be waiting for him with his share of the money after the concert."

"Only an idiot would trust you," Fletcher agreed.

"Precisely. Now, if you would be so kind as to join me outside, I'd like you two to take a short walk."

Suki's heart began to pound furiously in her chest, and she swallowed hard. "Where are we going?" she asked, trying not to sound as terrified as she felt. Fletcher put a protective arm around her, his eyes hard and cold as he faced Luchek.

Luchek opened the door and gestured grandly. "After you," he said, brandishing the gun as they stepped reluctantly into the hall.

He led them to a side exit and waved them outside into the freezing cold. They all walked silently to the trail until they came to the darkened ski lift, looming huge and empty in the night.

"This is as far as I go," Luchek announced. He gestured to one of the lift chairs. "Now get in. Both of you."

Fletcher hesitated. "I don't ski," he said, stalling. "Besides, it's very cold out. I could catch my death . . ."

"Precisely." Luchek smiled. "Now get in." He waved the gun at them.

Suki tugged at Fletcher's arm. "Come on," she begged. "I'd rather brave the elements than that gun." She climbed in without looking at Luchek, and Fletcher followed suit, his face set in a murderous glint.

"Don't be too sure of your choice, young lady," Luchek said as he threw the switch to start the lift. "It's about thirty below at the top of the mountain. It should take you about an hour and a half to walk back down, if you don't freeze first. And by that time, I'll be long gone."

The lift jerked upward, and Suki wildly clutched Fletcher's hand. Up they went, shivering fiercely in the wind. Fletcher turned boldly and gazed back down at Luchek, who was still at the controls.

"So long." Luchek waved. "If it's any consolation, no detective ever came as close to thwarting me as you did."

The lift rose into the air, abruptly ending any further conversation. "Well, that's a consolation, isn't it?" Suki said bitterly, trying not to look up to the dizzying top of the mountain, where she knew the winds would be ten times as biting as they were now. She forced herself not to panic. "I think we'll be able to walk down as long as the trail isn't too icy," she said. "Unfortunately, in weather like this, the trail is almost always icy. I just hope we can stay warm enough to survive the ride up."

"Just keep close to me," Fletcher said tersely as a stiff wind assailed them from nowhere.

Suki began to panic in spite of her effort. "I've heard that if you concentrate and think warm, it helps," she babbled.

Fletcher put his arms around her and began rubbing vigorously. Then he reached into his pocket and pulled out two envelopes.

"What are those?" she asked.

"Tickets to Acapulco. I thought if we looked at them, they'd help us think warm." He shivered convulsively, and clenched his teeth together.

Suki looked down at the tickets and tried to smile. "You—you really did expect me to go, didn't you?"

"We can be on that sunny beach in one short week. Just think, Suki. The temperature there is a hundred degrees warmer than it is here."

Suki tried to nod bravely, but another strong wind tore at them, eroding her courage. "Oh, Fletcher, let's not kid each other," she cried. "We could die up here." She wanted to bite her tongue out the moment she said it, but it was too late.

Fletcher seized her and kissed her icy lips with fierce determination, until she actually felt her circulation returning. They were halfway up the mountain, and by now the cold was taking its toll on her ears. She put her hands over them and squeezed. It was hopeless. She was being mercilessly, methodically frozen, and there wasn't anything she could do about it. Fletcher was watching her keenly, his shoulders shaking from the cold.

"Don't give up, Suki," he commanded. "You can't. Come on, where's your fighting spirit?"

She closed her eyes and shook with cold. "We'll never make it. And there's nothing you can say to change that."

"Are you sure?" he demanded, refusing to let her sink into total despair. "Let me take a shot at that."

"Go ahead," she said, fighting against the rising tide of panic that threatened to overcome her. She had to keep sane, at least. If she *was* going to perish up here, let it at least be from exposure and not from pure fright.

He was looking at her intently. "Suki . . . do you remember that first day we met in the elevator?"

She opened her eyes, but she could only nod once and shiver.

He hesitated, gripping her shaking hands in his. "Do you believe in love at first sight?"

Suki faced him dumbly, comprehension dawning slowly. "Really? You mean . . ."

"You caused me the biggest conflict of my career," he went on, his words biting into the cold. She looked into his eyes and saw something there that she hadn't seen before—or had she ever really bothered to look?

"You mean . . . you mean trusting me?" she asked shyly.

"I mean loving you." A bolt of warmth rushed through her, making her forget the cold for a moment. "It beckoned me and mocked me at every turn. I was crazy, trying to deny it, wanting to see you . . .I couldn't think straight on this case. Everywhere I went, you were there, haunting me."

Tears sprang to her eyes, and she blinked them back, afraid they would freeze on her cheeks. "Oh, Fletcher," she whispered. "If only you had told me."

"How could I? You had driven me mad. I went out of my way to try to prove you were innocent. So much so, that I was more interested in you than in this case. It's a wonder I could solve it at all."

She smiled slowly, her wit returning. "You had some help," she reminded him.

"Which brings me to an inevitable conclusion," Fletcher surmised. The wind howled around them as they approached the top of the mountain, and he pulled her even tighter to him. "I need a partner."

Suki gazed up at him, her breath creating clouds in the air. "What—what do you mean?"

"A full-time, lifetime partner. You know, fifty-fifty, and all that."

She trembled, not entirely from the cold. "What are you saying?"

"I'm not saying," Fletcher said. "I'm asking."

"Asking?" Suki could see the disembarking station up ahead. They were almost to the top. Her courage and her energy returned in full force. She looked at him in wonder. "Fletcher Colman, are you actually asking me to marry you?"

He nodded, holding her firmly against his body. "For richer or poorer, in sickness and in health, in safety and in peril. I love you, Suki, and I need you. I want to spend my life with you."

"This is certainly a hell of a time to ask a girl," she said, burying her face in his coat.

"I know, I know, but I thought it would get your attention. I had to take your mind off our—er, current situation."

She laughed, actually laughed up there at four thousand feet in the freezing air, trembling wildly in Fletcher's arms. She knew that she loved him immensely, loved his fire, his energy, his passion—if only they could live long enough to make it down this mountain!

She could think of only one way to keep warm the last several yards to the top. "Kiss me," she whispered fiercely. He obliged her readily, and their lips met in a storm of love and passion and determination that carried them through the last excruciating feet.

The lift came to a halt with a sudden bump, and they opened their eyes cautiously. The chair rocked hazardously in the riotous wind, but for an impossible split second all Suki felt was the warm glow of Fletcher's love. When she looked up, she saw that the chair was sitting safely on the platform.

They jumped out, and Fletcher stared all the way down the mountain to the empty parking lot next to the concert hall. The moon lit the dramatically sloping landscape of mountains and snow and sky. Everything was white and silently mysterious. For a brief moment, it was beautiful, but a sudden gust attacked Suki, returning her to earth. She knew that frostbite could set in at any time. "We'd better get started, Fletcher," she said hastily. "It's a long way down."

Fletcher wasn't listening. He was looking intently down the mountain. "That's our man!" he exclaimed. "Right on schedule, making his getaway." He pointed at the parking lot as a set of headlights beamed on suddenly. "That's got to be him."

"What difference does it make now? We could never catch him. We'd need a rocket to do that."

He turned and looked at her, a smile spreading across his blustered face. "Exactly," he said. "A rocket."

"Fletcher Colman, you aren't thinking what I think you're thinking?"

"You're brilliant," he said, kissing her. "Let's get moving. We'll surprise him at the pass."

"Oh, no," Suki protested. "I'm not going in that thing. Forget it."

"We have no choice! Do you want to freeze up here?"

"It's better than crashing into a tree at eighty miles an hour. Besides, it's dark. You can't possibly see the course."

"The moonlight will have to do. Besides, I've already run this course before. I could steer through it with my eyes closed. Come on. We'll catch him at the pass."

- 10 -

YOU'RE OUT OF YOUR MIND, FLETCHER. We'll be killed."

They were standing at the beginning of the icy runway, looking down the long moonlit run. Fletcher was double-checking the steering mechanism on the sled.

"Just remember to stay low and hold on tight."

Suki laughed nervously. "You don't have to tell me about the holding on part. I'll do that just fine. It's the turns that bother me. Should I lean left on a right turn and right on a left? Or is is the opposite?"

"Never mind that," he said, handing her a helmet. "When we hit those turns at eighty miles an hour you won't be able to lean anywhere. The centrifugal force on your body will be too great. You'll simply feel yourself being pushed down into the sled. That is, as long as I make the turns correctly."

She gulped. "And what if you don't?"

He looked at her and grinned. "That's where the holding on tight part comes in especially handy."

"I don't like this idea. I don't like this idea at all."

"You have no choice." He snapped his helmet on and checked hers. "Let's get moving. We have less than two minutes to cut Luchek off at the pass."

She looked down the path again, and then at the sled. "Here goes nothing." Getting in, she put her hands through the leather straps and squeezed.

"That's the brake," Fletcher said, pointing to a silver handle in back of her. "When I tell you, and only when I say to, I want you to pull that thing up with all your might."

Suki gazed up at him, frightened. "That will be my pleasure."

He tapped her helmet. "Okay, here we go."

He pushed the heavy silver-streaked sled along the track until it began to gain momentum. At the last possible second, Fletcher jumped in and they were on their way.

To Suki, the sensation was like a soft-bumping ride at the beginning of a roller coaster just before it gets to the top for the ride down. The cushioned leather seat warmed her slightly, although the adrenaline pumping through her body was also doing its share.

In no time at all, they were gaining tremendous speed. Suki could see the glistening, icy runway passing by her, reflected whitely in the moonlight. Up ahead, shadows played on the runway, making her wonder if Fletcher could really see anything at all.

"How can you see?" she yelled to him as the wind rushed past her face, making her eyes tear.

"I can feel it," he said.

Suki gulped. "But you said the moonlight was enough."

"I said I could do this run blindfolded, remember? Well, this is as close to it as I'll ever want to get."

Suki reached in back of her to feel for the handle of the brake. "Don't fail me now," she said.

The car was vibrating deafeningly, when Fletcher called out a warning.

"First turn coming up, right," he warned. "We'll pick up speed from this moment on all the way down."

"You mean it gets faster?" Suki looked ahead and saw nothing but darkness, when suddenly they sped around into the curve.

"Hold on tight!" Fletcher yelled.

"Aaahhh!" she screamed as the bobsled tore into the curve at breakneck speed, vibrating tremendously. They were actually going through it sideways. She could see the ground rushing by her left shoulder, and prayed that they wouldn't end up upside down. She could actually feel her body becoming heavier with the force, and then, thank heaven, becoming lighter once again as they emerged from the turn.

"How many more turns like that?" Suki called out frantically.

"No more like that," Fletcher yelled back as they sped faster and faster. Even the wind was powerless against them.

"Oh, thank God," Suki yelled. "I couldn't handle another one."

"I meant no more as easy as that one," Fletcher said. "That was nothing. It gets worse after this, and more dangerous. Get ready, here comes the next one. On the left!"

Suki had no time to prepare. They shot into it like a speeding bullet. "Fletcher!" she screamed. Again they were sideways, but this time moving even faster. It was as if the curve were a giant slingshot propelling them out. When at last they were moving right-side up, Suki found her voice. "How many more of those?"

"Five more," he yelled back.

"No, please, I can't take *any* more."

"You'll have to, here we go. Hold on."

They came out of that turn so fast that the sled was now rocket-propelled, whizzing by trees and objects that were only blurs in a white haze of nightmarish proportion.

"Another turn up ahead," Fletcher warned. "After that there's just hell's curves and we're home free."

"But you said four more—" She never finished the sentence as they once again smashed into a turn at breakneck speed. By now the velocity was so great that even the vibrations had steadied. Somehow, she took this turn calmly. It had all begun to take on an unreal quality. She allowed the force to pull her into the safety of the sled, and she looked up at the exact angle of the turn to see a beautiful moon shining down on her. It reflected off Fletcher's helmet and back at her. Then reality struck as they came back out and barreled downward at eighty miles an hour.

"Here's our fastest track," Fletcher yelled, trying to project his voice above the noise of the runners.

"We're making great time, but hold on. In five seconds, we'll be at hell's gate."

"What about the other three turns?" Suki yelled back. "You said three more."

"And they're all in hell's gate," Fletcher screamed. "Three in a row, one right, and two lefts. Now hold on and let me concentrate. I can't recall where they are exactly."

"What? Are you crazy?" She reached for the brake.

"Don't touch that brake," Fletcher warned. "You'll kill us."

"Not if you don't first."

"Almost there," he called back. "If we make it through this, will you marry me?"

"We're about to die, and you want an answer?"

It was too late to say anything more. "This is it!" he yelled. "Hold on for dear life."

That was exactly what she did. The right turn wasn't so bad, but the two lefts were horrifying, especially the second. Fletcher missed his mark coming out of the middle curve as something banged against the sled, making it ring like a bell.

"We hit a tree branch on the track," Fletcher screamed. "Hold on."

The sled was running dangerously close to the top of the wall of the curve.

"We're going over," Suki screamed.

"Not if I can help it. Hang on."

All Suki remembered was the constricting fear in her throat as she actually saw over the top for one sickeningly dangerous second. For that split moment in time, the surrounding countryside was open to her vision—a pastoral view marred by a speed of eighty miles an hour. Then they dropped safely back down and came out of the final curve heading for the finish line.

"We made it!" she screamed, her relief flooding through her. "We made it!"

"Get ready to brake," Fletcher ordered, still in command. "When I say the word."

She grabbed the handle, waiting for his signal to pull. Even without the brake, she could sense that they had slowed somewhat, but were still doing about fifty. She could see ahead to the finish-line banner blowing in the wind. Off to the left was the ski lodge, and on the right was the frozen lake.

"Should I brake?" Suki called out hopefully.

"Not until we're across the lake," Fletcher said.

"Lake? What do you mean, across the lake? There's no path across the—" Suddenly, it dawned on her. "Oh, no, you can't. You mustn't."

"I have to. It's the only way to beat him to the only road out of the valley. Hold on very tight and lean left."

She now knew exactly what he had meant about cutting Luchek off at the pass. In the next instant, Fletcher turned sharply to one side of the track, and then, with all his might, he drove the sled up and over the other side.

For a brief moment, Suki was weightless, a rocket careening through the air. She remembered screaming, and then they bumped down so hard that she was almost thrown out of the sled. She felt Fletcher's hand pulling her sideways.

"We made it!" he yelled as joyfully as a kid. " The rest is a piece of cake."

When Suki regained her senses, she was speechless. The sled was flying across the icy lake, bumping and vibrating as Fletcher easily maneuvered it toward an embankment on the other side.

"Now!" he called to her. "Pull the brake!"

She pulled with all her might, sending a flurry of snow up around them. The vibrations were earth-shaking. At first, it seemed that the brake wasn't having any effect at all. The sled continued to head for the embankment. "It's not working!" she cried.

"You're doing fine. Now hang on. We're going into that snowdrift."

A moment later, they hit the other side of the lake, scattering snow and powder in all directions. When at last they had stopped, Fletcher turned and lifted her out of the sled. It was fortunate that he did, because she couldn't have moved by herself. She was as limp as a rag doll.

"We're here," he announced jubilantly.

Suki was dizzy, and she stumbled into his arms. "We're where?"

"Believe it or not, we're standing on the only road out of town."

She couldn't believe her eyes. Sure enough, the asphalt beneath her feet was a road.

And with no time to waste, a pair of headlights was coming into view, speeding toward them. The car was going too fast to stop, but Suki wasn't thinking straight. "Oh, look, a car!" She began waving her arms. "Hey! Stop!"

Fletcher pulled her out of the way just in time. They both landed in an embankment just as the car slammed into the sled. The sound of glass and metal meshing and breaking was followed by the sound of a horn blowing out of control, piercing the night silence. When she looked up, she could see there was a man hurt behind the wheel, his head fallen forward onto the wheel.

"We have to help him!"

"Wait, Suki," Fletcher warned.

She ran over in spite of his warning, and reached through the broken side window to examine the inert man behind the wheel. She pulled his head back, abruptly stopping the horn, and froze at the sight.

"Luchek!"

He wasn't really injured at all. He smiled maliciously at the success of his deception and lifted his gun, pointing it straight at her.

"Well, well, so we meet again," he said snidely. "That James Bond tactic was most impressive." He looked over the steering wheel at the sled that was embedded in his front end. "What a shame. Now I'll have to hitch a ride to the airport."

Fletcher made a move toward him, but Luchek shoved the gun right up to Suki's head. "No farther, Colman, or she gets it."

"It's too late for you, Luchek. Face it, you're finished. I told you before, I called the police. Sooner or later, they'll be coming right up this road."

"You don't really expect me to believe that old ploy again, do you?"

Fletcher shrugged. "Suit yourself."

"That's exactly what I intend to do." Luchek got out of the car and held Suki's arm as he inched sideways. Reaching into the back seat without taking his eyes off her, he took out the suitcase full of money. "When it comes to this much money, it's never too late to try anything."

Suki scarcely dared to breathe, but she found that

anger was helping her to keep under control. She and Fletcher has risked their necks getting down that mountain. Who the hell did Luchek think he was to interfere now? She had half a mind to stop Luchek herself, but the gun was quite real and very menacing.

"As soon as you see a car coming, flag it down," Luchek commanded. "Once I'm in, I'll let the girl go."

"Fair enough," Fletcher said calmly, walking to the side of the road. It wasn't long before a car came barreling toward them. Fletcher waved his hands frantically until the driver saw him and pulled off to the side.

"Got a problem, buddy?" the driver asked.

Luchek moved forward, concealing the gun from the driver's sight.

"Could you give me a lift?" Luchek asked cordially. "We've had a slight accident."

"I can see that, bud. Sure, hop in the back."

The driver reached over and popped open the back door.

The man's voice was very familiar, but Suki couldn't quite place it. She felt Luchek's grip loosen.

"Good-bye, Mr. Colman," Luchek said as he moved away from Suki. Without taking his eyes from Fletcher, he got in and closed the door. "Take me to the airport, immediately." Luchek's voice was muffled through the closed window, but Suki could still hear the conversation.

"Sorry, I can't oblige you, fella."

Suki watched as Luchek held up his gun and pointed it at the driver. "To the airport," Luchek repeated, "or else I'll . . ." His threatening words were lost as he discovered that there was a heavy plastic partition between the front and back seat of the man's car. His gun drummed against it several times as he became fully aware of his circumstances.

"Nice going, Spalding."

Suki's eyes widened. "Detective Spalding?"

"At your service, miss."

In his panic, Luchek tried to open the door, but he couldn't. "There are no doorknobs in here," he shouted.

"That's the idea, bud," Spalding said. "I call this car my prison on wheels. Works great, too." He tapped on the plastic partition. "Bulletproof," he explained.

Suki approached him, stunned. "But how did you know to come out here?"

"I got a call from security. Some damn fool stole a bobsled and drove it down the course in the dead of night." Spalding turned around and looked at Luchek. "I have to hand it to you, mister. I watched your performance through binoculars. That was an Olympic-class run you just performed up there. But you could have got killed."

Just then sirens could be heard in the distance.

"Ah, the police," Fletcher said. "Better late than never."

Suki turned to him, trying desperately to piece it all together. Everything was happening too fast for her to comprehend. "Then you really did call them?" she said, gaping.

Fletcher merely smiled. "This job was getting a little too dangerous for me to handle. So I called in reinforcements."

For the first time since the shock of seeing Luchek

had paralyzed her, Suki began to be aware of the cold once again. Cold meant feeling, reality. She welcomed it. As she watched the police cars heading closer and closer, and saw Luchek trapped helplessly in the backseat of the car, a brimming sense of relief overcame her. She fell back against Fletcher, her breath coming in long, grateful gasps.

"Say you didn't lose those tickets to Acapulco, did you?" she asked.

He put his arms around her and held her close. "Honeymoon in the sun," he assured her, stopping right there to kiss her deeply and fully.

"Wait a minute," she said slyly, pulling back. "I never said I would marry you."

"Well, will you?" He looked boyish all of a sudden, earnest and hopeful.

"I don't know," she said, teasing him. "I don't know if I could stand such a dangerous life. But ask me again in Acapulco."

- EPILOGUE -

SUKI LAY BACK LUXURIOUSLY on the towel, letting the warm, soothing sun caress her skin. "This is heaven," she murmured drowsily. "Sheer heaven."

"Glad you like it," Fletcher murmured back, equally drugged by five days of indulgence. A full five minutes passed before he spoke again. "Would you like to go in and have lunch now? Or would you rather shower first? Or would you like to shower, make glorious love for an hour or two, and then have lunch?" He sighed. "Really, these decisions are too much for me."

Suki pondered for another minute. "I think I'll take choice number three."

He rolled over so that the long side of his body was aligned with hers, his arm flung over her on the sand. "Which one was that?"

"The three-stop tour. Shower, love, lunch." She opened one eye lazily and grinned. "Let's go."

She leaped up suddenly, fooling him, grabbed her towel, and began to run across the white sand back to the hotel.

"Hey, wait a minute!" he called, chasing after her.

Fletcher's long strides caught up with her easily, and he grabbed her in an armlock, pinning her to his side.

"Where have I seen this hold before?" Suki asked, laughing. "Oh, yes, that day you almost mashed poor Zeebo at my showing."

"He recovered nicely," Fletcher said, still holding her fast. "And he's got the best of it, I must say. His new client turned out to be a smashing success."

Suki's face glowed as she remembered the major showing in New York that Zeebo was planning for her. He had sold two more of her sculptures at auction, and she had garnered national attention.

Fletcher released her, and she spun around in his arms, her hands lacing around his neck. "You see," he said, "everything worked out after all. I told you it would."

"Ah, hindsight, hindsight," she chided lightly. "You weren't so sure when Luchek was holding a gun to our heads." She had been teasing him all week, but somehow it seemed appropriate. After all, she'd had to bear the weight of his suspicion while she was busy falling in love with him.

Fletcher cocked his head to one side. "But I was sure about you."

"Oh?"

He pulled her closer until their noses were almost touching, the mocking glint gone from his eyes. "I was sure I was in love with you. And I'm still sure." His voice became quiet and intense. "And you still haven't given me an answer, Suki."

Maybe it was the sun, ever-healing and ever-merciful. Or maybe it was the five days of sheer pleasure, free from worry and strain. They had enjoyed five solid days of complete trust and companionship, their rapport so effortless that they had often communicated without any words at all. Whatever it was, Suki knew suddenly that she couldn't put off the truth any longer. Fletcher's blue eyes were luminous and bright, demanding a response.

"I think you've punished me long enough," he said sternly, crushing her against him. "And don't deny that that's what you've been doing. Didn't I declare myself up in that ski lift in the freezing cold? Didn't I save you from Luchek? Didn't I—"

"Enough!" she cried. "You're right, I've been an unforgiveable tease. But you know, a girl doesn't like to be asked such important questions when she's in danger of losing her life. It really isn't fair."

He released her abruptly and fell to one knee in the sand, his arms outstretched, imploring. "My dear Suki," he began gallantly. "I love you madly with all my heart. Will you kindly do me the honor of becoming my wife?" His face changed comically as he clasped his hands over his heart. "Please?" he added beseechingly.

Suki laughed and tumbled down into the sand with him. She took his face in her hands and held it as she gazed into his wonderful blue eyes. "I love you," she whispered, her eyes brimming with happiness. "And I guess I'll have to marry you, or I'll never live it down."

"Are you sure?" he asked seriously, his eyes flickering on the brink of certainty.

She nodded once, her face radiant with joy. "Very sure." They kissed slowly, cementing their promise.

"There's just one thing I'd like to change," Suki said tremulously.

"What's that?"

"That three-stop tour you mentioned a minute ago. Shower, love, lunch, I think it was . . . Why don't we skip the first stop and head straight for the second? My priorities seem to have changed."

He stood up and lifted her masterfully in his arms, cradling her against him. "Best idea you've had all day."

COMING NEXT MONTH

FIRE UNDER HEAVEN #382 by Cinda Richards
Did Annemarie Worth and David Gannon fall in love during the month of terror they endured together? She says no, but he says yes...and he'll move heaven and earth to prove it!

LADY INCOGNITO #383 by Courtney Ryan
Who *is* the mystery woman who leaves Chad Delaney holding her Las Vegas jackpot? Chad's search for whimsical, vulnerable Alex Duffy leads to a love-filled odyssey across the Arizona desert.

SOFTER THAN SPRINGTIME #384 by Frances West
Past betrayal formed Jo Rossi's bitter opinion of the filthy rich. Now, forced to work with wealthy photographer Michael Travis, she's afraid to trust his easy charm...and unable to resist his captiv ating kisses...

A HINT OF SCANDEL #385 by Dana Daniels
When UFO investigator Darcey Dennison shows up on his Missouri ranch, Trey Jones finds he's got a lot more to worry about than an invasion of "little green men." Suddenly the whole town's talking romance, and Darcey seems destined to capture his heart.

CUPID'S VERDICT #386 by Jackie Leigh
When homespun farmer Jake Coltrane and wisecracking Atlanta municipal judge Vivian Minnelli collide—under *most* unusual circumstances—they emerge fighting mad...and irresistibly, powerfully attracted!

CHANGE OF HEART #387 by Helen Carter
The depth and vibrancy of Alex Stratis' new play strikes a chord deep within actress Marla Travis... but Alex's own sensual chemistry offers soul-stirring possibilities Marla's been afraid to face.

Order on opposite page

	ISBN	Title	Price
___	0-425-09285-2	**FRENCHMAN'S KISS #347** Kerry Price	$2.25
___	0-425-09286-0	**KID AT HEART #348** Aimeé Duvall	$2.25
___	0-425-09287-9	**MY WILD IRISH ROGUE #349** Helen Carter	$2.25
___	0-425-09288-7	**HAPPILY EVER AFTER #350** Carole Buck	$2.25
___	0-425-09289-5	**TENDER TREASON #351** Karen Keast	$2.25
___	0-425-09381-6	**BEST OF STRANGERS #352** Courtney Ryan	$2.25
___	0-425-09382-4	**WHISPERS FROM THE PAST #353** Mary Haskell	$2.25
___	0-425-09383-2	**POCKETFUL OF MIRACLES #354** Diana Morgan	$2.25
___	0-425-09384-0	**RECKLESS GLANCES, STOLEN CHANCES #355** Lee Williams	$2.25
___	0-425-09385-9	**BY LOVE BETRAYED #356** Ada John	$2.25
___	0-425-09386-7	**LONG ROAD HOME #357** Jean Fauré	$2.25
___	0-425-09437-5	**WHERE ENCHANTMENT LIES #358** Beth Brookes	$2.25
___	0-425-09438-3	**CODY'S HONOR #359** Carole Buck	$2.25
___	0-425-09439-1	**REBEL HEART #360** Molly Thomas	$2.25
___	0-425-09440-5	**DARK SPLENDOR #361** Liz Grady	$2.25
___	0-425-09441-3	**FOREVER KATE #362** Samantha Quinn	$2.25
___	0-425-09442-1	**FORTUNE'S HUNTER #363** Frances Davies	$2.25
___	0-425-09508-8	**HEAVEN CAN WAIT #364** Dianne Thomas	$2.25
___	0-425-09509-6	**CONQUER THE NIGHT #365** Karen Keast	$2.25
___	0-425-09510-X	**SUN-KISSED HEARTS #366** Kit Windham	$2.25
___	0-425-09511-8	**SWEET TEMPTATION #367** Diana Mars	$2.25
___	0-425-09512-6	**TWICE IN A LIFETIME #368** Pat Dalton	$2.25
___	0-425-09513-4	**CREATURE COMFORTS #369** Adrienne Edwards	$2.25
___	0-425-09609-2	**RUGGED GLORY #370** Cait Logan	$2.25
___	0-425-09610-6	**HANKY-PANKY #371** Jan Mathews	$2.25
___	0-425-09611-4	**PROUD SURRENDER #372** Jackie Leigh	$2.25
___	0-425-09612-2	**ALMOST HEAVEN #373** Lee Williams	$2.25
___	0-425-09613-0	**FIRE AND ICE #374** Carol Katz	$2.25
___	0-425-09614-9	**ALL FOR LOVE #375** Sherryl Woods	$2.25
___	0-425-09690-4	**WHEN LIGHTNING STRIKES #376** Martina Sultan	$2.25
___	0-425-09691-2	**TO CATCH A THIEF #377** Diana Morgan	$2.25
___	0-425-09692-0	**ON HER DOORSTEP #378** Kay Robbins	$2.25
___	0-425-09693-9	**VIOLETS ARE BLUE #379** Hilary Cole	$2.25
___	0-425-09694-7	**A SWEET DISORDER #380** Katherine Granger	$2.25
___	0-425-09695-5	**MORNING GLORY #381** Kasey Adams	$2.25

Available at your local bookstore or return this form to:

SECOND CHANCE AT LOVE
THE BERKLEY PUBLISHING GROUP, Dept. B
390 Murray Hill Parkway, East Rutherford, NJ 07073

Please send me the titles checked above. I enclose ______. Include $1.00 for postage and handling if one book is ordered; add 25¢ per book for two or more not to exceed $1.75. CA, IL, NJ, NY, PA, and TN residents please add sales tax. Prices subject to change without notice and may be higher in Canada.

NAME ____

ADDRESS ____

CITY ______________________ STATE/ZIP ______________________

(Allow six weeks for delivery.)

SK-41b

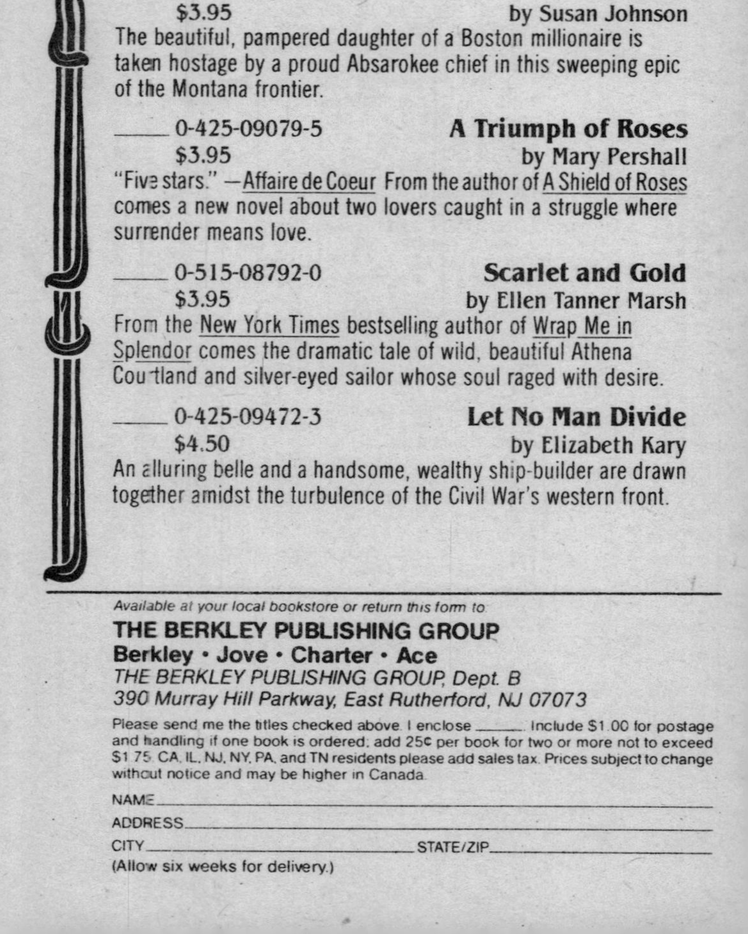